Dear Diary,

Today I picked up a hunk as he was escaping his own wedding. I know—doesn't sound like anything Eden Whitney, prim librarian, would do, right? Well, it gets even better. Right now I'm sitting in the honeymoon suite awaiting my—gulp—"husband." Not really—we're just pretending to be married. You see, Riley—that's his name—has just been jilted, and a lot of important people are expecting him to show up here with his wife. So here I am, so to speak.

God, I must be crazy. My heart is pounding a mile a minute. How am I going to pull this thing off? I've never even shared a glance with a man this sexy—much less a honeymoon!

Well, I was looking for an adventure. Who knows? Maybe I'll even land myself a husband....

Till tomorrow,

Eden

Dear Reader,

If you take a look at the back covers of our two books this month, you'll notice that each one features a multiple-choice question. I don't know about you, but taking tests was not exactly my favorite thing to do back when I was in school. (I don't think we'll discuss just how long ago that was!) However, I took both these quizzes and had no trouble at all coming up with the right answers, and I don't think you will, either.

Carla Cassidy's *Pop Goes the Question* is very aptly titled, because it's inside a helium balloon that Mary Wellington finds the note that's going to change her entire future. What I'd like to know is this, however: How come the only notes *I* ever find are discarded shopping lists? Of course, I've never been whisked away by a just-jilted groom, either, though that's exactly what happens to the heroine of Christie Ridgway's *Follow That Groom!* I think I'm going to have to start taking my life cues from these books!

Anyway, read and enjoy them, and then come back next month for two more terrific novels about meeting, dating—and marrying—Mr. Right.

Yours (truly),

Leslie J. Wainger
Senior Editor and Editorial Coordinator

Please address questions and book requests to:
Silhouette Reader Service
U.S.: 3010 Walden Ave., P.O. Box 1325, Buffalo, NY 14269
Canadian: P.O. Box 609, Fort Erie, Ont. L2A 5X3

CHRISTIE RIDGWAY

Follow That Groom!

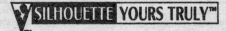

Published by Silhouette Books
America's Publisher of Contemporary Romance

For Jen and Cynthia

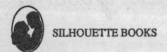 SILHOUETTE BOOKS

ISBN 0-373-52038-7

FOLLOW THAT GROOM!

Copyright © 1997 by Christie Ridgway

This edition published by arrangement with Harlequin Books S.A.

® and TM are trademarks of Harlequin Books S.A., used under license. Trademarks indicated with ® are registered in the United States Patent and Trademark Office, the Canadian Trade Marks Office and in other countries.

Printed in U.S.A.

About the author

When I was a little girl my parents told me I could be anything I wanted. I wanted to be a writer.

After college I became a technical writer and computer programmer. After creating pages of technical information and line after line of computer code, I discovered I wanted to be a writer of fiction.

Following the birth of my first son, I quit my job outside the home and fit time for reading into my day. After many, many pleasurable hours, I knew I wanted to be a writer of romance novels for Silhouette Books.

I live in Southern California with my supportive husband of twelve years and our two very patient sons. I'm active in Romance Writers of America and volunteer in my sons' school. And any spare moment between writing, car pooling, mommy-ing and wife-ing, you'll still find me reading.

Books by Christie Ridgway

Silhouette Yours Truly

The Wedding Date
Follow That Groom!

1

Riley Smith ignored his grinding tension headache and fumbled again with the striped bow tie of his tuxedo. Hell. How come a guy, who could shake a Sahara-dry martini and blend a daiquiri to a lady's taste, couldn't tie a simple bow?

Behind him, from the door of the church's small dressing room, he heard a sound. *Great.* Struggling once more with the ends of the bow tie, he watched in the mirror, waiting for the doorknob to turn. Probably one of his upper-crust in-laws-to-be, checking up on the groom. No doubt an inability to make a perfect bow tie would be proof of his less-than-blue blood.

When the door didn't open, Riley smoothed his damp palms down his pant legs and attacked the striped noose again. He must've been wrong about the noise. But even as he tried to concentrate on the tie, an ominous feeling crept over him. A feeling like an unseen pair of eyes was watching him, like a silent bomb was ticking away, like— He turned, his gaze sweeping the small room. And then he saw it, a tightly folded note that lay on the floor beside the door, his name scrawled across it.

The text of the note was surprisingly brief, given the chatty nature of the author, but it held all of her usual breezy charm.

Riley,
By the time you read this I'll have slipped out the back door—I'm in love with someone else and can't marry you. Do me a terrifically huge favor, darling, and tell everybody you've called it off. Daddy will kill me if he knows I've done this *again!*

"'Again?'" Riley echoed.

A tangle of anger and rejection slid from his heart to take up residence in his gut. Gulping a bracing breath, he forced himself to reread the note. Then he crumpled the paper in his fist.

"I should have known," he muttered. He really should have realized that when push came to shove, the youngest and most pampered daughter of the blue-blooded Delaneys of Rancho Santa Fe would never marry the likes of a Riley Smith.

With a quick gesture, he undid the top button of his pleated tuxedo shirt. At least he could give up on the tie. And at least his raging headache had miraculously disappeared.

But now what? At this moment, seven monkey-suited Delaney men lined the altar. And in the church's vestibule waited a mountain of pink hoop skirts and hairspray. Seven bridesmaids looking like those cro-chet-skirted Barbie doll toilet-paper concealers. He was going to have to tell somebody that the bride had called off the parade down the aisle.

Do me a terrifically huge favor, darling, and tell everybody you've called it off. That line of the note resounded in his brain with all the breathy insistence of his ex-intended. Oh, hell. It would serve her right if he read the entire damn note aloud to all five hundred guests.

But then he'd have to watch the understanding dawn in their eyes.

They'd recognize that the bride had finally come to her senses and dumped him. At long last, they'd think, she'd realized that bartender Riley Smith just wasn't good enough for her.

Lost in thought, he rhythmically squeezed the balled-up bad-news note. If he took the blame, as requested, he could at least salvage his pride. In fact, they'd all wonder why a Delaney wasn't good enough for Riley Smith. A tight smile curled his lips.

Wouldn't that be a sticky piece of humble pie for his almost in-laws to swallow?

Riley shoved the note into his pocket. His knuckles bumped against the velvet box that cradled the platinum wedding band, and his fingers closed around it. He'd throw it away. Open a window and toss it as far as—

No. He'd keep it, as a reminder of a lesson he should have learned long ago.

A reminder that Riley Smith should stick with his own kind.

A reminder that Riley Smith was not a marrying man.

With that decision firmly in hand, he took a deep breath and made his way out of the dressing room. He walked down the thickly carpeted church hallway, mentally using the eeny-meeny-miny-moe method of selecting the person to break the news to. When he bumped into the kindly, but scatterbrained minister, he decided against him, though Riley took his "Bless you, son," with gratitude. He had a feeling he was going to need every blessing he could get.

The hallway led to the vestibule, and at the doorway he lingered. From his position he had an oblique view of the church's sanctuary, pews filled with what looked like all of San Diego's upper crust. The vestibule itself was crowded by the gaggle of bridesmaids and various other members of the wedding party. Beside a huge floral arrangement stood the father of the bride, the aristocratic line of his nose rivaling the beak of the bird-of-paradise flower that was the focal point of the display.

Eeny meeny miny moe. It made ironic sense that he'd break the news to the man who'd insisted on the prenuptial agreement. Riley squared his shoulders and took a step toward his almost father-in-law, Lawrence Delaney. No sense in putting off the announcement.... But then Lawrence slipped into the sanctuary and bent to talk with an elderly man in the last pew.

Riley ran his gaze around the room and tried again. *Eeny meeny mi*— "Ouch!" He looked down at his stinging shin.

"Gotcha, goon." A ten-year-old Delaney, the designated bags-of-rice tender, smirked and swung her beribboned basket toward his other shin.

Riley jumped back. "Hey, cut that out."

"I don't like you." The rice tender shook her Bo-Peep curls that matched her Bo-Peep dress. "None of us like you."

"Oh, yeah?" Riley grimaced. If he didn't have other things on his mind, he'd have a better comeback.

"And even though you made a bunch of money in cheap bars, you're dumb," the girl added. "Everybody says that. My cousin couldn't have picked a bigger loser."

Over the head of the little darling, Riley caught sight of his mother-in-law-to-be. *Ex*-mother-in-law-to-be, which was sounding better all the time.

He strode toward her, eager to get the task over with. The rice tender dogged his footsteps, swinging her basket dangerously close to his legs. "Evelyn." Riley touched the Pepto-Bismol-colored sleeve of the mother of the bride.

"*Now* what?" She sent him a harried look over her shoulder. "Mother, Mother." She signaled toward the bride's crotchety grandmother. "One of the ushers is ready to take you in now."

Grandmother Delaney stomped over, poking her cane into the carpet with each step. "Not Gerald's son, I hope. I cannot abide that boy's after-shave. Or that overbite of his." She pursed scarlet-lined lips. "I told them they picked a shoddy orthodontist."

"Well, Mother—"

Riley tried again. "Evelyn."

She shot him another look. "What are you doing here? Go get up front where you belong."

"Evelyn—"

"Listen to me, Riley. This isn't the time to be wandering around. Even a young man with your lack of background—"

"Evelyn, I've decided there isn't going to be a wedding."

"—should know that. For goodness' sake, we rehearsed..." Evelyn's eyes widened. *"What did you say?"*

Riley ignored the basket whacking his shins. "I've decided there isn't going to be a wedding."

Evelyn clutched at the air, and when Riley tried to offer support, she batted his hands away. "Lawrence!" she called. And more loudly, "Lawrence!"

Mr. Delaney apparently heard the warbling cries and rushed out of the sanctuary to his wife's side. "What, Evelyn? What?"

She grasped the lapels of his gray coat. "Riley's calling off the wedding! He's jilted our poor baby!"

Lawrence's country-club tan paled. "Oh my God. The expense...the *embarrassment*...." He caught his wife as she swooned against his chest.

Riley leapt forward. "Let me help—"

"Get out!" Propping up his wife, Lawrence sent Riley a vicious look. "Haven't you done enough? Just get out!"

Riley took a step back, nearly tripping over the rice tender. "Wedding wrecker," she accused.

The bridesmaids buzzed like a hive of angry bees, and their disturbed hums reached the back pews of the church. People twisted around, big-bowed hats and stern patriarchal faces turning his way. Like a wave, Riley watched the news of the kiboshed wedding roll to the front of the church.

Lawrence's voice rose again, over the muttering crowd. "Get out!"

Riley hesitated. Should he just leave it like this? Just walk out? But the sight of the clench-fisted grooms-men striding down the aisle cinched his decision.

"Time for the good guy to exit stage right," he muttered.

"Searching for adventure," Eden Whitney whispered to herself, steering her Buick sedan past the stately palms on Date Boulevard in the direction of the coastal highway. Each mile she put between herself and the Whitney Library made the notion seem more possible. She couldn't dim her carefree smile.

At a stoplight, she made a cursory check of the back seat. Her garment bag and overnighter were stacked side by side, packed with everything she'd need for two weeks on the road.

Still waiting at the long light, she attempted to smooth the cream linen of her long-skirted dress. The June heat had pressed wrinkles into the originally crisp fabric, but she'd thought the lacy collar and loose A-line had suited her last prevacation duty—the volunteer luncheon she'd hosted in the library garden that afternoon.

Approaching another red light, Eden noticed the long line of cars ahead of her and deliberately turned onto a side street to avoid the traffic. She smiled, congratulating herself on the small impulsive act. That was what this trip was all about. If the traffic bothered her, she'd find another route. If a road beckoned, she'd travel on it as far as she liked. If an exciting possibility presented itself, she'd press down on the accelerator and take on the possibility at full speed.

Up ahead, across another intersection, a large church stood on the right. Struck by its serene beauty—cool white walls, tall stained-glass windows rising toward gently arching palm trees—Eden eased on the gas pedal. A block-long limousine hugged the curb, a Just Married banner strung across its rear window. As she watched, a man approached the white vehicle.

Oooh, she thought. *Now that's a man.*

In a pearl gray tuxedo coat with tails, his white shirt unbuttoned at the throat and the ends of his bow tie fluttering free, the man wore his dark hair long. He strode toward the limo, exuding attitude. Eden braked behind the limit line of the intersection, a hundred feet from him.

There wasn't a car behind her, so she planted her foot firmly on the brake pedal and just stared. It was the attitude that intrigued her. Attitude that was infused in his walk and in the set of his shoulders. He didn't swagger, he just walked with—with—attitude. And she, Eden Whitney, Special Collections Librarian of the illustrious, yet incredibly stuffy Whitney Library, possessed a real admiration for attitude.

People with it spent their days in ways other than caretaking the family treasures. People with attitude reveled in adventurous evenings out, unlike librarians whose rare dates were with men preapproved by Daddy in the same way banks preapproved her for a credit card. Cash in the bank—check. Steady job—check. Prestigious family, boring life-style, unexciting future. Check, check, check.

From the curb, the attitude man leaned across the rear window of the limo so he partly obscured the Just

Married banner. What was he doing? He seemed to be looking inside.

For a clearer view, Eden used the button to completely lower the passenger window. Had he left something locked in the limo? She didn't see the driver around anywhere. Maybe the bouquet was in there, or the rings. She bet he was the best man sent after the—

She shook herself. Here she was, daydreaming again. Making something up about someone else's life instead of living her own. No more! That was the point of this whole vacation.

"Searching for adventure." She repeated her newly adopted mantra again, and shifted her foot from the brake to the accelerator. The car eased forward through the intersection.

She passed the back bumper of the limo and with a sidelong look through her open passenger window, checked out what the gorgeous man was doing. He leaned away from the limo just as she glanced over. At the end of the calligraphied Just Married banner, her attitude man had emphatically lettered a big, black, blazing NOT.

Eden's eyes widened. What was this? In her surprise, she touched down on the brake, halting her Buick in the street, right beside the limo.

Before she could move along, the man looked toward her, his expression puzzled. "Having trouble?"

Embarrassed at being caught staring, Eden froze, her summery linen dress suddenly feeling like a sauna suit. She shook her head, then transferred her gaze to the steering wheel. *How silly I must look.*

"Do you need some help?" Now his voice came through the passenger window.

She looked up, and through the window met his eyes. They were gold. Whiskey gold. Old gold. I've-been-around-a-thousand-years-and-a-thousand-blocks gold. He had attitude, a charming smile and old eyes. Beneath her dress, a shiver of excitement tickled her spine.

"Need some help?" he asked again.

She opened her mouth to answer, but before a sound came out, he turned his head over his shoulder and glanced back at the church. Across the rising green lawn, the double doors opened and women dressed in picture hats and men in suits began flooding out. Leading the mob was a girl swinging a huge basket and an elderly woman with a cane and a sour expression.

"Oh, hell," the man muttered under his breath.

Eden took that as her cue to move on. But just as she accelerated forward, the attitude man strode around the front of the car. Bumper met tuxedoed leg with a soft, but definite tap. Eden slammed on her brakes and turned off the engine.

"*Oh.*" She pushed open her door and jumped out of the car. "Are you all right?"

The man casually brushed his leg. "Just fi—" A walnut-size net bag flew past his startled face and burst against the street, spilling white rice. "Oh, hell," he muttered again.

Eden whirled toward the church. The girl was tossing another net bag up and down in her palm, while the sour-looking old woman pawed through the basket. The little girl took aim and another bag of rice sailed through the air. Both Eden and the man ducked behind her Buick.

"How dare—" Eden began. The bag thumped against the hood of the car and rice rained over the two of them. She looked at the man. "—they?"

Shrugging, he shook his head. "Let me cut you a deal, hon. I won't sue you for hitting me if you give me a ride outta here." Another rice bag exploded against the car, and more grains fell over their heads. "Please?" He gave her a rakish grin, but his eyes held a hint of desperate vulnerability.

Eden gulped, unprepared for the appeal. *What in heaven should I say?*

The man's golden gaze sent a wash of heat across her cheeks. She might be a staid librarian, but she wasn't stupid. If she was looking for adventure, this moment—no, this *man*—couldn't be a better advertisement for it if he sported an eye patch and a hook for a hand.

Another secret rush of excitement sizzled down her spine. Not trusting her dry throat, she nodded in response to his inquiring eyebrow.

He grinned. Another rakish, adventurous grin. In seconds, they'd slid into her car, leaving him in the driver's seat.

"You mind if I drive?" he asked.

More rice skittered against the windshield. "The Padres oughtta sign that kid up," he grumbled.

Eden smiled. "Go ahead. You drive."

He turned the key she'd left in the Buick's ignition. Under his hands her normally sedate sedan roared to life, an animal recognizing its mate.

He gave her an appreciative look from his golden eyes, and nodded his head. "Let's do it!"

Heart pumping like a teen's on prom night, Eden buckled herself in. And as the car gave an eager jump then raced off, Eden wrapped her arms around herself and felt like the queen of the ball.

Riley cut the engine of the Buick, not surprised to find himself in the parking lot of the first bar he'd ever bought. He'd driven here unconsciously. Over the plain door cut in the stucco building, he checked out the bar's sign and noted the neon loop of the *y* in Riley's No. 1 was on the fritz again. He made a mental note to have it repaired. While the patrons of this bar didn't like anything fancy, *he* didn't like the place to look seedy.

The woman beside him unclasped her seat belt and he turned his head to watch her gracefully slide out of the car. What a good sport. Not every woman would take on a desperate guy. Must've been the tuxedo.

He grinned to himself. She probably didn't know what to think. Any self-respecting woman probably hated seeing a guy defacing a Just Married sign. He climbed out of the driver's seat and stood looking at her over the roof of her car.

"Well, uh, thanks." For the first time, he took a good look at her. She was young, with long brown hair, a small, straight nose and the rest of her face covered by huge dark glasses. Her body was even more disguised in a dowdy white dress.

She gave him a tentative, sweet smile.

And suddenly he didn't want to be alone.

Oh, if he went inside, Stu would be behind the bar and would happily set him up with a round. But he'd have to explain a lot, a hell of a lot, that he didn't feel like going into right now.

"How about joining me for a drink?" The words popped out of his mouth before he'd even thought the idea through, but he didn't regret them. It was an unwritten rule in Riley's No. 1, or in any of the six other bars he owned, that a guy with a date was left alone. The only kind of question a man with a woman needed to answer was what he was having.

She seemed to be hesitating. He didn't blame her. She didn't know him from Adam. "My last name's Smith." He jabbed his thumb in the direction of the sign. "They'll vouch for me in there." He grinned. "They have to. I'm the boss. I'm Riley."

She cleared her throat and held out a slender hand, fingernails short and unpainted. "I'm Eden. Eden Whitney. Very nice to meet you, Riley."

He smiled at the prim introduction, and gave the small hand a reassuring shake. "Let me buy you a drink."

She hesitated again, but then seemed to make up her mind. With a nod, she slammed shut the passenger door and he led the way to the entrance. As he held the door, she tossed back her hair and went in, removing her sunglasses with one hooked forefinger.

Behind her, Riley admired the rippling mass of sunshot brown hair, its bright threads quickly dimmed as she entered the dark interior of the bar. Her sensible shoes clicking against the hardwood floor, she passed between the first few tables, then halted, as if uncertain where to go. Signaling to the astonished-looking Stu for a couple of beers, Riley passed her and led the way to a dime-size scarred table in the nearest corner.

They slid into opposite chairs, giving Riley another look at her face. ''Your eyes are blue,'' he said, making the discovery as he shrugged off his tuxedo coat. Okay, so it was a clunker of an opening line, but it was the first thing to pop into Riley's head. Above a little nose, Eden Whitney had a pair of long-lashed blue eyes. The rest of her face sort of disappeared behind her fall of hair, but she had a good mouth. He looked again. A real good mouth, with a short upper lip and a full lower one.

''Mmm.'' She fidgeted in her chair, smoothing her long skirt over her knees.

He guessed she wasn't much of a talker, which suited him just fine.

Her small hands folded themselves into a ladylike igloo, which she studied with seriousness. The pulse in her throat, just bared by the neckline of the frumpish dress, fluttered nervously. The shallow hollow mesmerized him, and he found himself thinking of— *Naah.* God, what was wrong with him? He'd planned to be saying his ''I do'' about now, not scoping out some strange woman's neck.

Stu came by with the beers, sending all sorts of messages and asking all sorts of questions with his bushy eyebrows, but Riley ignored the communication. He drained half his beer in one gulp, and watched Eden take a swallow of hers.

''So, uh, thanks for the ride,'' he said.

She smiled. Her perfect teeth made him a little nervous and put him in mind of the bride who'd just ran out on him.

''You out for a drive?'' he asked, trying to distract himself from the image.

She took another dainty sip of beer, and he saw her try to stifle a grimace. "I'm out for an adventure," she stated emphatically.

In that dress? "Aah."

"Excitement," she added, her gaze leaving her beer for his face.

Riley smiled; he just couldn't help himself. This woman looked like the kind who came from a vanilla world and considered choosing chocolate ice cream an adventure.

Unlike his kind. The unwelcome thought came, unbidden. His kind had backgrounds that were pure, trashy hells. Backgrounds that you could only try to wash away with money and success.

A tide of anger and rejection rose in him again and he concentrated on forcing it back down.

"So what happened?"

Riley looked up, startled by the first question she'd asked of him. "Uh…" He downed the rest of his beer, and signaled behind his back for Stu to bring over another. "I was supposed to get married today." Another twinge, a quick knife edge of discomfort, slid over his skin.

"You don't look like the marrying kind."

And that's the truth. Riley grinned at her, the momentary flash of pain disappearing as quickly as it had come. "You know, you're absolutely right."

He noticed that her beer was down to a foamy quarter inch. "Let me order you another." He gestured toward her mug.

She shook her head, light tendrils drifting up from her temples then floating back down. "I've got to get going."

"You're meeting someone? Have to be some-place?"

She shook her head again.

"Then stay for another." He took a swift glance around the room. He couldn't say for sure, but he had a funny feeling that Stu had made a few phone calls. This place should've been deserted on a Saturday afternoon, what with the basketball finals over and the baseball season caught in midseason doldrums. But where there had been empty bar stools when he'd walked in, there now sat a crowd of regulars. Guys who should've been home mowing the crabgrass.

"I could use a buddy right now." He tried out his most charming smile.

She frowned. "There seems to be plenty of people here to talk to."

That's the problem. What he really could use was an excuse not to explain to those "plenty of people" why he was here drinking beer, and not dancing at the wedding reception. He tamped down another wave of rejection, then straightened in his chair, inspired. "A dance. Right now I could use a dance."

"I don't know." She had a worried look in her eye, and she darted a glance toward the door, as if gauging the distance. "I'm not ... I mean ... dancing—"

"Hey, if I stomp on your feet you can sue *me*." He rose from his chair and held out his hand. "C'mon, honey."

She grimaced, but stood up herself. "You don't look like the toe-stomping type."

He grasped her hand. "Sounds like you have me pegged." The flesh of her fingers was smooth and warm. The contact felt good, and he entwined his fingers between hers. A tremor of awareness edged up his arm and he headed it off before it went anywhere near his heart.

He led her to the jukebox beside the parquet dance floor and fished two quarters from his pocket—his knuckles bumping against the wedding-band box— and slipped the coins into the jukebox. After a moment's debate he punched up a Springsteen classic. Eden looked to be in her twenties, young enough to maybe prefer Pearl Jam or Hootie and the Blowfish, but the folks that hung out here preferred the hard-driving, hard-living beat of the Boss.

The song started, the rhythm entering his blood like a hot shot of tequila. He pulled her into his arms. She felt good in his embrace, too. Soft and sweet. And she smelled good, so he inhaled the light scent of her perfume as he started leading her in a country two-step modified to a rock-'n'-roll beat.

Eden stumbled a bit, and he gripped her tighter, pulling her hips against his so she could catch the rhythm of his movements. "You like the Boss?" he murmured into her ear.

She stiffened and pulled a little away. "Pardon?"

He put his lips against her ear again. "Do you like the Boss?"

"Well, uh, Riley, I hardly know you."

That took him a minute, until he remembered how he'd introduced himself. Then he laughed. "I didn't mean *me*. Yeah, I'm the boss here at Riley's, but I meant the Boss, with a capital *B*. Bruce Springsteen."

Her cheek felt warm against his. "Oh. Of course. Yes."

He laughed again, his arm sliding down her back to gather her close once more. He had a lot to thank this woman for. Here he was, *laughing,* on what could have been the gloomiest day of his sorry life. "So tell me about this adventure you're looking for."

"My bags are packed and I'm heading up the coast."

A vague uneasiness penetrated Riley's good humor and he tried pushing it away. He didn't want to think about anything but the armful of sweet warmth he was cuddling against his chest.

"I'll see how far I get. I have a general plan, but I'll take whatever road looks like an adventure."

Somebody had stuck some more quarters in the jukebox, and the beat of the next song was heavy and throbbing, like a lover's pulse. Riley slowed his shuffling feet, but didn't loosen his hold on Eden.

She looked up at him, and he stared into her face. He watched her take a breath then swallow, and his gaze followed the movement from her parted lips down the smooth muscles of her neck. *Her neck, again.* He looked back into her eyes.

Her voice came to him faintly. "I'll take on the open road," she said. "Under the sun, under the moon. Stay anyplace that strikes my fancy...."

Her voice faded away. He breathed in her flowery scent. His eyes traced the concentric rings of her sapphire irises. "Blue eyes," he said, trying to ignore the curling heat in his body and concentrate on what she'd been saying. Open road...stay anyplace that strikes my fancy...stay anyplace. Under the sun. Under the moon. *Stay anyplace. The moon.*

Oh, hell. He stopped short, his abruptness causing Eden to slam against him, the full length of her body smack-dab against his. "Oh, hell," he said aloud. "Now I'm without a bride for the honeymoon."

2

---◆---

Eden's heart pumped wildly against Riley's hard chest. The wailing sax notes of the jukebox song didn't drown out the sound of her breathing in her own ears.

Excitement.

The air shimmered with it.

Her blood sizzled with it.

Never before had she felt such an intense, immediate, fiery attraction to a man.

"No bride," Riley repeated, his voice tense. "No honeymoon."

Eden's fizz of excitement flattened. While she was feeling the effects of sexual chemistry experiments, he was thinking about a honeymoon that wasn't to be. She pushed against his chest and he immediately loosened his hold, looking down at her as if suddenly remembering he held someone in his arms.

"Excuse me," he said abruptly. "I need to make a call."

He left her on the dance floor and disappeared into a doorway behind the bar. The song they'd been dancing to petered out in a disappointing chorus about love gone away and a final plunk-plunk-plunk of sad piano notes. Eden sighed.

So much for her first adventure.

She squared her shoulders and headed back for the corner table. She shouldn't have agreed to come in for a drink. But she'd never been inside a *bar* bar before, one that wasn't just a waiting area for a fancy restaurant. It had seemed to be a day of firsts.

First day—first hour!—of her first vacation alone.

First attack by rice-throwing wedding guests.

First pick-up of a man.

She grimaced and grabbed her purse off the tabletop. Next time she'd remember to choose someone other than the groom.

She looked toward the door Riley had disappeared through and didn't see a sign of him. Though it went against a lifetime of training, this time she wouldn't make her goodbyes to her host. She would just quietly leave. Not that he would be the least likely to miss her.

She was ready to be on her way, all right, as soon as she found her car keys.

Eden unearthed two battered breath mints and a pencil stub from the bottom of her purse before she remembered that Riley had been the one driving, and presumably the one who had pocketed the keys. With gloomy resignation, she pulled out the chair and sat back down. She inspected her closely cropped nails while she waited. She could only hope he'd walk back through the bar on his way out of her life.

"Can I bring you something?"

Eden lifted her head and looked up at the bartender. His bristly eyebrows rivaled the giant caterpillars she'd recently seen in one of the pictorials of the library's rain forest collection.

Eden shook her head. "I'm just waiting for Riley." She hesitated. "He's still around, isn't he?"

The bartender grunted. "Holed up in his office." He narrowed his eyes. "You *aren't* the bride, are you?"

"No." Eden didn't allow herself even the tiny luxury of such a daydream.

"Just checking." The bartender pulled out the opposite chair and lowered himself into it. "Riley hadn't brought her around, but judging by his other women over the years, I, uh...uh..."

"Just didn't think she could be me?" Eden ignored the heat crawling up her cheeks. No one had to tell her that Riley "Attitude" Smith would never marry a woman as plain and dull as she.

"So what happened?" the bartender asked.

"I don't really know," Eden answered. "The guests were pitching rice at him when I happened by."

The bartender looked relieved. "Lucky SOB."

Eden's eyes widened. "Lucky?"

"A guy like Riley shouldn't saddle himself with a wife. What's he need one for?"

"Companionship? Love?"

The caterpillar eyebrows drew together. "He's got all the companionship right here and at the other bars he owns around town. As for love... Riley himself says that's a bunch of hooey."

"So why was he getting married?" Eden couldn't stop herself from asking.

"Dunno. He's been doing strange things lately. Bought himself a hotel up the coast. Says he wants to branch out from the bar business."

Eden nodded. "Diversification." Her father claimed that diversification was the key to Grandpapa Whitney's buildup of wealth.

The bartender snorted. "Dumb. What could be a better way to spend the day than watching ESPN and pouring beer?"

Eden didn't feel qualified to offer a counterargument. She had spent the past few years cataloging books and catering to library donors and elderly volunteers. "Maybe he just wants something different."

That was what she wanted—no, needed. After waking up one morning and watching the maid set out another in a long series of beige dresses, she'd realized she was twenty-six going on middle-aged.

Daddy hadn't understood at all. He'd granted her request for a vacation, then immediately called the family travel agent to arrange a place for her on a Caribbean cruise. He'd even suggested any one of several eligible young men as a potential traveling companion who could conveniently segue into a fiancé. He didn't say that, but it was all too clear.

But she'd been clear with Daddy, too. For the first time in her life she'd gone against his I-know-what's-best and insisted on her own vacation. She'd promised herself her own adventure, which she'd get on with once she received her missing keys.

In his office, Riley slammed down the phone and guzzled the last of the beer he'd grabbed from the refrigerated bin beneath the bar. "Why doesn't anyone answer?" he asked aloud, staring down the bikini team member featured on the calendar pinned to the wall.

Of course, she didn't answer, either.

Riley squeezed the sweaty bottle of beer and let his temper rise. He'd kept it in check until now, but a guy had a right to be ticked off on a day like this. Not only had he been dumped at the altar, but now he couldn't contact his partner. Miguel should be at their newest financial venture, a small resort hotel named the Casa Luna, preparing for tomorrow's visit from *Getaway* magazine. But instead, both the business lines and even the reservations line just kept ringing.

Damn. Riley slid off the edge of the desk and wrenched open a few more studs of the scratchy, starched tuxedo shirt. He better get up to the Casa ASAP. *Getaway* was expecting to cover a honeymoon—his honeymoon—and he and Miguel would need to brainstorm another way to keep the prestigious magazine's interest. The story and photo spread they'd promised almost guaranteed the Casa Luna's success.

Slapping open the office door, he thought about grabbing another cold one from the bar, but decided against it. He couldn't try to go numb until he had the *Getaway* situation straightened out. Another wave of anger swept over him, and he shoved his hands in his pockets to keep from punching the wall. After that, he'd have himself a wedding night—with a bottle of whiskey instead of a bride.

He strode across the dance floor, fishing in his pockets for his car keys and pulled out—hers. Eden's. *Oh, yeah,* he thought, another spike of anger flashing through him. His almost brother-in-law had driven him to the church that morning.

She rose from the corner table as he approached. "You're going north, didn't you say?" he asked abruptly.

She blinked, then nodded. "Up the coast."

"Great. I need a ride." All he wanted was to get to the Casa as quickly as he could, no questions asked.

She blinked again. "Um, um...um..."

Riley spun toward the front door, ignoring her little sputterings. He needed that ride. While this situation wasn't her fault, she was female, and the way he suddenly saw it, the female sex owed him. Big-time.

Her Buick engine was already revving by the time she slid into the passenger side. He slung his arm over her seat as he reversed, and he noticed her flinch away from his fingers. Guilt gave him a momentary stab as he drove quickly away from the bar.

"I promise I won't bite," he said.

"The promise of a carjacker?"

He felt another stab of guilt and shot a look at her. But she didn't really appear afraid. "I think you have to be out of the car for this to be carjacking. This may be more like a kidnap."

"Ah." She didn't seem to appreciate the fine point he was making.

"Listen, I'm sorry, but I've got to get up the coast."

"Couldn't you have appropriated someone else's car?"

Riley sighed. "Stu walks to the bar, and those other guys... I just didn't want to explain." Right now his insides were a little tender and he didn't feel like having his bar buddies, or anyone else for that matter, poking around at them.

"Having to explain what?"

He'd obviously been wrong earlier about her being the silent type. "That would be explaining."

"Ah," she said again.

He sighed. "Look. I own this hotel up the coast. Nobody's answering the phone and I need to get there. Okay? Is that enough?"

She just looked at him.

He sighed again. "I have a lot riding on this hotel, okay? And this mess today maybe just screwed up a big chance we have to make a go of it."

"What? The wedding guests had reservations?"

"Very funny." He didn't feel like talking any more about himself, the damn wedding, the hotel. He didn't want to explain that making a success of the Casa Luna would mean he could thumb his nose at all those who'd stuck up theirs at him.

"Let's talk about you," he said, to distract her.

"Me?" she squeaked.

He liked that. Squeaking women weren't the type to grab a guy's—guts—and give 'em a big twist. "Yeah, didn't you tell me you were on a vacation?"

"Yes, a vacation."

"Or no, it was an adventure, you said."

In the afternoon sunlight he could see a blush rush up her neck. He liked that, too. "Well, yes, an adventure," she agreed.

"What kind of adventure? Whitewater rafting? Camping trip through the Sierras?"

She shook her head and mumbled something.

"What was that?"

She stared out her side window but spoke more clearly. "A trip to the California missions."

"Huh?"

Her voice rose defensively. "I'm taking a driving vacation and stopping by each of the California missions I haven't visited before. San Juan Capistrano, San Juan Bautista and—"

"San Juan the Most Boring Vacation I've Ever Heard." He looked over at her, puzzled. "You're putting me on, right?"

"Why would you say a thing like that?"

Riley blinked, and gave her another good look. Unless she'd discovered the Fountain of Youth, this woman looked to be around twenty-five. And while the clothes and hair were without style, and the face without any trace of makeup, the basic structure of the whole package wasn't unsound. A shocking thought came to him. "You're not a nun, are you?"

A telling silence rose from the other side of the car.

God, it all made sense. The formless clothes, the mission vacation. Jeez, he'd been dancing with a Sister! He shifted in his seat uncomfortably. She'd even sort of turned him on!

"Listen, Sister, I'm really sorr—"

"I'm *not* a nun." Her voice sounded strangled.

Now it was his turn to be silent. "Oh," he said after a long pause. "It was just a thought."

He shut up after that. Which led him back to dwelling on the hellacious day he was having. He thought up long, exquisite tortures for the snooty Delaney clan, particularly that rice-throwing bratty little kid. And his ex-bride-to-be—he couldn't even think about her without his neck heating up to near-combustible temperatures.

"Riley?"

He grunted in acknowledgment, his brain occupied with a fantasy about that prenuptial agreement and his ex-father-in-law-to-be. The man who'd said he'd never been able to say no to his daughter, even when she went slumming for a husband.

"Do you think I should go somewhere else for my adventure? My second choice was a trip through the Gold Country. You know, all those tiny towns and interesting characters. Joaquin Murieta, Black Bart..."

Riley shook his head. "Honey, those men aren't adventures. Those men are dead."

She bristled. "I'm not looking for *men*."

Riley rolled his eyes. "Yeah, right."

Her spine hit the back of her seat with a sharp thwack. "Why don't you believe me?"

"Because I'm thirty years old? Because I'm a man myself?"

"What's that supposed to mean?"

"It means that in my experience, and not-so-limited experience, if I do say so myself, the kind of adventure a woman is looking for has nothing to do with historical landmarks and everything to do with a man."

More telling silence from beside him.

"You can't deny it," he said flatly.

She squirmed. "I think all single people are looking for love."

He snorted. "Don't get me started on love." A discussion of that tender feeling would likely end up with him talking about the day-destroying little note that had been shoved beneath the door. And he'd promised himself not to talk about *that*.

"Well, *my* adventure is not about men. It's about being out on my own, doing what I want, getting away from the books—"

"Are you a student?" Maybe she was younger than he thought.

"No, I'm a librarian."

Riley laughed. "I should have known."

"What's that supposed to mean?"

He made a gesture in her direction. "How shall I say this? The Marian the Librarian primness."

"Primness?" she echoed.

"Yeah, you know."

"No, I really don't know."

She didn't sound mad, just curious, so he tried to elaborate. "You know, the old lady clothes, the hair thing."

She was quiet again. He looked over and realized that his last few words had been less than diplomatic. "You have pretty hair." He tried to backpedal. "But..."

"But?"

He grimaced. "But it just sort of hangs there." *Great job, Smith.* He groaned inwardly. *Take the woman's car and her ego, too.*

"Well, thank you." There was hurt in her voice. "Thank you very much." With a big *humph,* she crossed her arms over her chest. "And haven't you had a big day? Break one woman's heart and another woman's self-image."

"And what do you mean by that crack?"

"How do you think the bride felt when you refused to marry her?"

Her accusation was like a spark to the tinder of Riley's already-bad day. "That's another problem with you intellectual types. You *librarians*. You think you know all the answers."

"What do you mean by that?" she asked.

He sent her a furious look. "I was just being honest with you. Just like that little note I received five minutes before the ceremony. The one in which the bride jilted *me.*"

Eden bit her lip and slid her gaze toward Riley. Ever since he'd dropped the bombshell about being jilted, they'd maintained an uncomfortable and ominous silence. She wanted to know how much farther to his hotel, but didn't feel up to another conversation.

She sighed. She didn't do well with men. On a business basis she had no trouble, but when it came to social occasions, she never seemed to get it right.

Though this didn't really qualify as social, she supposed. Yes, this situation with Riley definitely defied normal classification.

She pushed her hair behind her ears, then pulled it over her shoulders, then forced herself to stop fussing with it. Riley's plainspoken, "But it just sort of hangs there" shouldn't have surprised her. She hadn't done anything with her waist-length hair in years. She knew it was unstyled, but she didn't know what to do about it. The last hairdresser she'd approached had been reluctant to cut the mass when Eden couldn't say what she wanted done with it. So she'd settled for another one-inch trim.

And about her clothes... Well, the same applied. She lacked the knack for stylish dressing, just didn't know how to go about selecting the right things for herself. Her mother had died when Eden was eight, and Daddy had instructed a succession of housekeepers to keep her well dressed. It was surprising but true that even the most exclusive stores stocked an expensive selection of boring clothing.

"We'll be there in about ten minutes."

Riley's voice cut into her thoughts, and she sent him another guarded look. She could hardly believe he'd been jilted. As she watched, he ran a hand through his hair. The dark strands settled in tousled disorder against the collar of his white shirt. It gave Eden shocking thoughts of rough-and-tumble sex on crisp white sheets. She squirmed in her seat.

"What?" he asked.

Her eyes widened. "What what?"

"You're wearing a funny little smile."

"I am?" She primmed her mouth. "And was it any more stylish than my dress?"

He grimaced. "Ouch. You got me. Can you maybe forgive me?"

She shrugged.

"I'm sorry, Eden." He sighed. "This hasn't been my best day, and we're about to part company. I'd like us to say goodbye on good terms."

She nodded. "Let's call a truce."

"Truce." He held out his hand.

"Truce." She shook it.

And then he didn't let go. She felt his callused palm against hers, and just like when they'd danced, she didn't feel the least inclined to pull away. Like fierce competitors, every nerve in her wrist raced off to be the first to tell the rest of her body how good his touch felt. Her lips went suddenly dry, and she licked them.

Riley looked over just as her tongue swiped her lower lip.

His fingers squeezed hers. "Nice" was all he said, and then he let her go.

Eden's hand flopped into her lap and she waited for her pulse to slow. In vain.

Riley turned off the coastal highway and took a narrow winding road toward the beach. Another left, right, left, and then a discreet sign: Casa Luna and a long driveway framed by blooming white oleanders and scarlet bougainvillea. Shortly, the foliage thinned enough for her to see a charming grouping of Mediterranean-style white-stucco-and-red-tile-roofed buildings surrounded by tropical plants and closely cropped grass.

The driveway curved and Riley slowed as they approached the largest of the buildings, a four-story structure with Juliet balconies and a small sign on the first floor that said Office. Eden didn't see any staff members or guests.

"Where is everyone?" Riley muttered.

In the afternoon sunlight, the place appeared lush, waiting, almost breathless.

The car halted, and Riley opened his door at the same moment that Eden did hers. Salt-scented air washed over her face, and without the distortion of the car's tinted windows, the colors of the buildings and flowers appeared even more startlingly vivid. As she stepped onto the springy grass, an immediate sense of buoyant well-being filled Eden. "It's beautiful, Riley."

His brows drew together. "Thanks," he said, obviously distracted. "Thanks very much." He spun around, took a step toward the office. "Where *is* everybody?"

In the distance, Eden heard the distinctive strains of mariachi music. Not a cucaracha-type song, but a melodious strumming that spoke of happiness and love. Eden smiled. "That music sounds live."

A strange expression crossed Riley's face. "It does, doesn't it?"

The music drew closer. Eden turned in its direction, a narrow brick path between two of the buildings. Riley seemed frozen, another peculiar, almost nauseated expression on his face. "Eden, get back in the car," he said quickly.

"What?" She frowned. "But I love this music." Even as she spoke, the first of the musicians appeared, wearing black pants with a white Mexican wedding shirt, and strumming a huge guitar.

"Damn." Riley's voice held a blend of humor and weariness.

Eden crossed to his side and put her hand on his arm. "Are you all right?" She took her gaze off the mariachi musicians that were forming a ring around them on the lawn and looked into Riley's face.

His gaze traveled down her face to her shoes, and back up. "You're wearing a white dress."

"Ivory."

He briefly closed his eyes. "I still have my tuxedo on."

She blinked. Why was he stating the obvious? She laid her hand against his cheek. Was he coming down with something? "Well, yes."

More people flooded the path the mariachis had traveled. Two dozen or more followed, most wearing uniforms, filling in behind the crescent the musicians had established.

A niggle of unease ran down Eden's spine. The people were all smiling at them. Big smiles. Congratulatory smiles. *Uh-oh.*

This time Eden was afraid to look into Riley's face. "I have an odd feeling about this, Riley."

"Me, too."

The strains of the hauntingly romantic song swirled around them. People still filtered down the path. Everyone continued smiling.

Eden couldn't believe that Riley wasn't doing anything. "Riley," she whispered, grabbing his hand to get his attention. "They think—they think—"

"I know," he said, his posture now relaxed. "Calm down. We'll just make the best of it and I'll straighten it out in a minute. It's good practice, and when they're done we'll all have a big laugh."

Suddenly, though, his spine straightened and tension radiated off him. "Oh hell," he muttered. "Now this isn't funny. The *Getaway* people came a day early."

Eden looked in the same direction as Riley. One last couple was traveling down the red brick path—a nattily dressed woman and a man with two cameras strapped across his chest, and another in his hand. He pointed it in their direction.

A cheer broke out from the crowd as two of the uniformed men unfurled a white banner with red lettering. Eden groaned, glancing over at Riley. " 'Congratulations, Mr. and Mrs. Smith'?"

He turned toward her, apology written all over his face.

"Kiss! Kiss!" the crowd yelled.

Time seemed to stop as Riley met her eyes. Those old gold eyes, full of reluctant humor and a warmth no man had ever regarded her with. Eden heard the clicking of camera shutters, and more encouragement from the crowd. "Kiss! Give her a kiss!"

The mariachis still played, more seductive sounds that seemed to root Eden's feet to the ground. Riley had another, new expression on his face. Tenderness? Regret? Uncertainty? And suddenly his eyes were very, very close.

"Kiss! Kiss! Kiss!"

"For some crazy reason, that sounds like a good idea," he said. And his lips descended.

3

What insane impulse had led him to kiss her? The thought blazed through Riley's mind and then he couldn't think anymore.

Eden's mouth—that "good" mouth he'd noticed in the bar—tasted as sweet as raspberries. Her lips trembled beneath his, and he parted them to inhale more of her delicious taste.

His blood began a heavy *chug-chug* through his body, and as he prolonged the kiss he cupped Eden's cheek, and then stroked down so he could feel the answering pulse beat at the base of her neck. She made a little sound in her throat, just a tiny noise that felt like a purr against his fingers, but it was enough to attune him to other sounds. He heard the final strum of a guitar, good-natured catcalls and the click-and-zip of a camera shutter being squeezed again and again. *Oh, hell.*

Riley forced himself to break the kiss and pulled the stunned-looking Eden against his chest. Her fingers dug into his biceps, and he hoped the little sting would clear his confusion. *Why did I kiss her?*

The mariachis began another song, and Riley ran a hand over his face, trying to wake himself to reality.

An accumulation of all the day's unexpected events must have rattled his brain. The beaming smiles of his staff, as well as those of the *Getaway* reporter and photographer, confirmed that they thought Eden was his wife. That damn kiss had sealed their mistaken belief.

Though his real almost-bride had never been to the Casa Luna, she had met his partner a few times. And by the look on the younger man's face as he rapidly approached them, Miguel realized that Eden was the wrong woman.

He gripped Riley's hand. "Congratulations, my friend," Miguel said heartily. And then in an undertone he added, "What is going on here?"

The photographer was still clicking away, so Riley pasted on a groomlike smile. "I didn't get married," he said through his teeth. "Why are the *Getaway* people here a day early? And what's with this spectacle?"

Miguel clapped Riley on the shoulder. "Just a little surprise we cooked up for you. At the last minute, *Getaway* decided they wanted to cover your arrival, and we decided to do it up right. So who's this?" He nodded toward Eden.

Riley performed a quick introduction. When Miguel kissed her on the cheek, Eden didn't blink an eye. She still appeared dazed.

Miguel put on his own welcoming smile and muttered, "What are we going to do? *Getaway* was expecting your honeymoon, and now they've got pictures of... of... what?"

Not one good response popped into Riley's head. "We better think fast."

Miguel's fake smile didn't waver. "Only two choices—we either kiss the magazine spread goodbye, or you just found yourself a new bride," he said in Riley's ear.

"Tell me something I don't already know." Riley had come to that same conclusion the moment he'd spied the *Getaway* reporter and photographer. Maybe, subconsciously, that's why he'd kissed Eden.

A new bride. He stared down at the woman he held against his side. Could they pull it off? *Getaway* had never asked the name of his intended.

Riley made a quick decision. "Miguel, can you spirit Eden and me away for a couple minutes alone?" Eden had said herself she was looking for an adventure. How long could it take to convince her that over a California missions tour a honeymoon won hands down?

"So what was that scene outside all about?" Hoping desperately to clear her head, Eden shook it. "Some kind of big joke?"

Riley shuffled his feet. "Uh, no joke." He gestured toward the tapestry couch in the living room of the luxurious suite he'd ushered her into, and tried grabbing her hand. "Would you like to sit down?"

Eden stepped away from him. "I'd like to know exactly what's going on." She put her hands on her hips. "And no touching or kissing. That's what befuddled me into following you in here in the first place."

"Befuddled?" Riley grinned. "I don't think I've ever had that effect on a woman."

"Hmm." Eden refused to commit herself further. She had no doubt that Riley had that effect on any number of women, but women too sophisticated, unlike her, to admit it.

"Okay, so you want to know what's going on...."

Eden bit her lip. Did she really? Since she'd first laid eyes on this man today, nothing had gone according to plan. Of course, she'd never expected to be kissed....

Don't think about the kiss. The memory sent a sweep of chills down her back. Probably because she'd never been kissed so softly, and yet so thoroughly. Mostly because she'd never been kissed by a man with attitude. She sighed. This attraction she felt for Riley was something that had to be squelched.

Or run away from.

"I think I have to go now," Eden said. This was the safest decision. "Don't bother with explanations. I just need my car keys and some directions on how to get back to the highway."

Riley grimaced. "Those missions are waiting, huh?"

Eden held out her hand. "Just give me the keys."

A brief knock sounded on the suite door, and at Riley's quick acknowledgment, a uniformed young woman carrying a huge fruit basket entered the room. "Good afternoon. These are for you two."

Eden suddenly found her hand captured. Riley brought her palm to his mouth. "Thank you, Lisa," he said, then brushed his lips over Eden's sensitive flesh.

She tried to hide her shudder from Riley and the bright-eyed Lisa who placed the basket on a side table then crossed to the room's draped windows. "Shall I open these for you? Or—" she gave them a knowing smile "—would you like the privacy?"

"Open—"

"Closed—"

Riley spoke at the same moment Eden did.

The maid giggled. "I'll let you work it out." As she left the room she sent them another sidelong look, her smile widening as Riley placed another gentle kiss on Eden's palm.

The door quietly shut, and Eden wrenched her hand from his loosened grasp. "Excuse me! I asked for the keys, not a kiss."

When he didn't make a move, she eyed him with determination and cleared her throat. "Riley, the keys."

He stuffed his hands in his pockets. "Sorry, but I passed them to Miguel. He was going to have the car moved to the valet parking area."

Eden sighed. "Okay. Just tell me where—"

Another knock sounded. Again Riley quickly invited in the intruder. This time, a young man in black pants and a black vest entered, carrying a tray with an ice bucket, champagne and crystal flutes. "A gift from the bar staff."

Riley smiled. "Thank everyone for me, will you?" He looked over at Eden. "Would you like a taste now, sweetheart? I know I would."

Why is he calling me sweetheart? Eden crossed her arms over her chest. "No."

With a maddening man-to-man shrug to Riley, the barman deftly opened the champagne and poured out a glass that he passed to Riley. "Are you sure you wouldn't like some, ma'am?"

Eden smiled. "No, thank you. But if you could tell me where I can find the valet parking... ?"

The man's eyebrows rose, and he looked over at Riley. "It's the covered structure to the right of the main building."

"Thank you very much." Eden nodded. "If you'll excuse me, gentlemen?"

Riley strode to her side, and grabbed her hand. "I'll be happy to take you on a tour, sweets."

What? *Sweets?*

He handed his champagne glass to the other man. "We'll be back to enjoy the rest of the bottle shortly." He hustled Eden toward the door.

"Don't count on it," she called over her shoulder.

"What are you trying to do?" Riley whispered as he led her from the sumptuous suite back outside into the warm afternoon. "Blow the whole thing?"

"*What* whole thing?" She sighed. "Oh, I forgot. I don't want to know."

Riley gripped her fingers tightly. "Miguel and I own this place. We acquired it just a few months ago."

Eden nodded, trying not to be distracted by the feel of his long, strong fingers separating hers. "Congratulations."

"*Getaway* magazine is here for a cover spread on the Casa Luna."

"*Getaway?*" Eden halted. She knew of the prestigious and influential travel magazine. As a matter of fact, it had recently published an article on the Whitney Library.

"Getaway," Riley confirmed. He pulled her down a lushly landscaped path that led away from the main building. The curving stonework suddenly opened onto a secluded black-bottom pool, complete with a waterfall and surrounding tropical plants.

"Wow." Eden sighed at the beauty of the spot. Not only was the pool cool and inviting, but the view from the deck surrounding it showed a sweeping expanse of sparkling Pacific.

Riley smiled. "There are three pools at the Casa Luna, but this one is my favorite." Suddenly he pulled her into his arms, setting his forehead against hers.

Eden blinked, and her heart started pumping. "Wha—"

"Shh. Someone's coming."

From behind them, Eden heard footsteps. Steeling herself against her quivery reaction to the muscled expanse of his chest, she lowered her voice. "Okay, I give up." She breathed through her mouth to avoid his delicious male smell. "I have to know. What are we doing?"

"Getaway is here to cover my honeymoon. That's the hook of the article. 'Owner In Love At His Own Resort,' or something like that." The footsteps faded away, and he lifted his head, then released her from his embrace. "We're safe now."

Safe now? Eden gaped at him. How could she be safe when her pulse was racing and every spot his body had touched hers still sizzled? Her brain started working again. "And you don't have a honeymoon anymore," she said slowly.

"And I won't have the *Getaway* exposure, either, unless I get a bride." She couldn't miss the significant look he sent her way.

Eden gaped again. "No." She held up her hands and waved him off. "No way."

Riley reached out and drew a finger along her cheek. "Why not? You said you wanted an adventure. They already assume we're married, anyway."

She ignored the heated shiver caused by his touch. "An adventure, yes, not a honeymoon. You'll just have to tell everyone they made the wrong assumption."

"Come on. You get a groom." He smiled. "And you've already admitted this place is beautiful."

Abruptly he pulled her into his arms again. For a minute she leaned against him, and pretended it was all for real. But she heard the footsteps, too.

"Wouldn't it be fun to be my wife?" Riley whispered against her ear.

Goose bumps spread down her neck. She heard music in her head—drums and chanting. A primitive call to adventure. Yes, this was her chance. "Really? You could see me as Mrs. Smith?" The thought was simultaneously exciting and terrifying.

His breath bathed her temple. "Will you do it?" The footsteps faded away, and again he released her.

With inches of distance between them again, oxygen finally reached Eden's brain. What was she doing? How could he think for a minute she'd agree? "This is silly. Of course I won't," she said in her best reference-books-cannot-be-loaned librarian voice.

He frowned, then spun to look toward the ocean. Minutes ticked by. Eden heard the rustlings of little creatures in the foliage, and the distant, raucous cries of sea gulls.

"You're probably right," he finally said, his voice resigned. "Nobody would ever believe it."

That comment is enough to make any self-respecting woman bristle. And Eden might be sheltered, but she *was* self-respecting. "And what's that supposed to mean?"

He shrugged. "Nobody would believe you married me. You're a librarian. You wear... You look..." He gestured vaguely.

I wear. I look. He'd already been through all that on the trip in the car. And suddenly, in a flash of wounded pride, she became angry. Really mad. "I could, too, be your bride."

He turned, inspected her up and down with a critical eye. "I don't know.... I need someone who people could see as my wife. Someone more reckless, impulsive."

Eden sniffed. Why, today she'd already taken several chances, made several spur-of-the-moment decisions, and he still didn't think she was good enough. "I could do it," she said stubbornly. *I think.*

He pursed his lips, apparently considering. "I need the whole enchilada, honey. Someone people could believe I'd marry. Someone who looks like she's hot in the sack. Someone a little *bad.*"

A heated shiver ran down Eden's spine. Oh, how she wanted, just once, to be a little *bad.* If only she could convince him.... She'd prove to them both there was more to Eden Whitney than dusty books and bookish looks. "Listen, I didn't want to explain myself before, but... but..."

"But?"

She thought fast. "But what I wear, how I look, is like a costume, you know?"

"A costume?"

"I'm a librarian. And I *do* like the job." She took a fast breath. "But I'm really just looking for some good times." The words rushed out.

His eyebrows rose. "Just a good-time gal?"

"Yes," she said recklessly. "That's it exactly. This is the look I need for work, to be taken seriously, you see, but the rest of the time... Well, just trust me. I could be the hottest bride a honeymoon ever had." As proof of her determination, she twisted her grandmother's plain wedding band off her right hand and slid it onto her left ring finger.

Eden heard more footsteps. Riley took a swift glance over his shoulder, and with a calculated decision, Eden sidled up against him. She slid her hands around the back of his neck. "See," she whispered, "this is the real me." Her heart going a mile a minute, she reached up and placed a tiny kiss against his square jaw. And then another.

Riley grunted noncommittally, but his arms came around her waist. Whether it was merely for the benefit of the Casa Luna employee walking by, she couldn't tell.

"The real me," she said again. The excitement of the whole idea made her voice husky. She kissed his chin this time, and then, to her own amazement, her tongue slipped out to lightly taste him. *Oh, goodness.* He tasted like salt, like skin, like *man.* "Doesn't this look and feel convincing?"

Riley grunted again, a longer sound this time, almost a groan. A thrill, of exhilaration, of power, sizzled through Eden's blood. She drew her hands down his pleated white shirtfront. "I can do it, Riley. We can pull it off." Another soft kiss to the underside of his chin.

More moments passed. She inhaled another breath of his scent, savored the taste of him on her tongue. "Say yes," she murmured, almost to herself.

"Yes." Riley's arms closed tightly around her.

"Yes?" Eden squeaked out. *Yes?* Her librarian sensibilities fluttered around her stomach in belated dismay.

"I think we can pull it off." He grinned. "You and me, Eden, my good-time, adventure-seeking, no-holds-barred bride."

No holds barred? Eden started trembling in reaction. She hadn't said *no holds barred.*

She'd agreed! Riley wiped beads of imaginary sweat from his brow. What a relief. He'd been a little surprised by her "just looking for some good times," but when he thought about it, it did make sense. No stuffy, primmed-up woman would rescue a guy from a rice-throwing mob.

So she was a librarian. That didn't necessarily mean she wasn't anything else. Come to think of it, she'd proclaimed from the get-go she was out for adventure. But what about the missions-tour vacation? How did that fit in?

Don't look a gift horse in the mouth, Smith. He had a bride. And he had a honeymoon. *Thank God.*

Holding her small hand tightly, he continued leading her on a tour of the Casa Luna. They walked past the other pools, the two cabana bars, the dining room, the small nightclub, and the secluded cottages that were the most popular of the Casa Luna's accommodations.

Pride rushed though him as he pointed through the lush foliage toward the steep-staired path leading to the beach. The resort was a significant step up from the bars he owned. While he felt his roots were with them, his heart was here. Success of the Casa Luna would mean he'd finally risen above his youth—when he'd lived in a world far from the beauty and serenity of this place.

"Where is everybody?" Eden asked as they passed two empty tennis courts. "Most of the people I've seen are people who work here."

Riley grinned. "'Behind closed doors...'" he sang softly.

Eden looked at him blankly.

"You don't get it?"

She shook her head.

"Ahhh. I think I left out something unique about the Casa Luna."

"And what's that?"

"*Luna* is moon in Spanish. Casa Luna is—"

"The House of the Moon," Eden finished.

He nodded. "This is a honeymoon hotel."

Eden looked surprised. "I thought that was only in the Poconos. So do the rooms have heart-shaped beds and bathtubs?"

Riley laughed. "This is honeymoon, California-style. Privacy and pools, beaches and even bands if couples want to visit our nightclub in the evening."

"You can keep the rooms full with only honeymooners?"

He shook his head. "It's not a requirement to get a room or cottage, it's just what we'd like to be known for. We even have special rates for second-timers."

"People on their second honeymoons?"

He shrugged. "Or, more likely, people on their second marriage."

Eden halted and pulled her hand from his. "That's a pretty cynical view."

He looked into her face. She was serious, earnest even, so he didn't laugh. Was he cynical about marriage? Of course. His own parents had never entered into that happy state, and for himself, well, he'd just been dumped at the altar, hadn't he? "I guess you're right," he said. "I don't think much about long-wedded bliss."

"So why *were* you getting married today?"

"That's a good question." The answer was somewhere, buried deep within those tender insides of his, but he didn't feel like delving for it. "Let's talk about something else," he said abruptly.

"Like what?"

Riley grabbed her unresisting hand and tugged her in the direction of their honeymoon suite. "Like how I'm going to pay you back for the whopping favor you're doing me."

"By the way," she said breathlessly, "exactly how long must this favor last?"

"Four or five days. The *Getaway* people will take a couple of pictures of us. Miguel and I will give them the lowdown on the Casa Luna."

She bit her lip. "What if they ask questions...what if they want to know more about me?"

"Don't worry." He refused to borrow trouble, not when he finally had the situation in hand. If necessary, he'd head off the *Getaway* team from probing too deeply. "They want a story on the resort, not us." He felt certain that the only one who'd want to know Eden better would be him.

He looked into her eyes, as deep and darkly blue as a sleepless night, and experienced a heated rush to the center of his body. Like the rush he'd felt when he danced with her. Like when he kissed her. Like when *she* kissed *him*. Yeah, he wanted to know her better.

But only in order to find an adequate way to thank her, of course.

"Do you really think you can pull this off?" Over the dinner cart he'd wheeled into the suite, Miguel regarded Riley soberly.

Riley lifted a cover and breathed in the aromatic rosemary chicken and new potatoes. "Of course."

Miguel didn't appear convinced. "What about her?" He nodded toward the bedroom.

Through the half-open door, Riley could see Eden take a stack of clothes from her suitcase. Though he'd changed into jeans and a T-shirt from the bag he'd packed and left at the Casa for his original honeymoon, she still wore the Bride-of-Nerd white dress. A kind of costume, he reminded himself. "She'll be fine."

"I don't know," Miguel said.

Something in his voice put Riley on edge. "What do you mean by that?"

"Just a few murmurings from the staff. They're a little surprised by your choice."

Riley shrugged, and checked the label on the bottle of white wine. "What's wrong with Eden?"

"I'm not saying there's anything *wrong* with her. She just doesn't look like the type who wants to play-act at marriage."

Riley craned his neck to get another view of her. In the white dress and the rippling long hair, he had to admit she didn't look much like the good-time girl she'd claimed. "She's out for an adventure," he told Miguel. "And we've got one for her."

"So in a few days she'll walk away from here?"

Riley nodded. "That's right."

"And in the meantime? How far are you going to take this 'honeymoon'?"

Riley's stomach dropped strangely. "We, uh, haven't really discussed it."

"Haven't discussed it? You didn't make it clear this was a honeymoon-in-name-only? That you don't want her to actually go to bed with you?"

Riley mumbled under his breath.

"What?" Miguel asked.

"Maybe I do want her to go to bed with me."

Miguel snorted. "Riley, you were supposed to marry someone else today. And now you're thinking about going to bed with a different woman?"

Riley tried feeling guilty. He tried conjuring up the face of the real bride. Neither the emotion nor the image materialized. "Miguel, I'm not thinking about anything but pulling off this honeymoon," he lied. "Believe me."

With a look of pure disbelief, Miguel exited the suite.

Riley frowned, staring down at the sparkling silverware on the dinner cart. He and Eden probably should set the ground rules for the honeymoon. And while her eyes, her smile, the body he'd sensed beneath the sacklike dress turned him on, he knew he shouldn't hop into bed with her. He might be a little wild, a little bad, but he wasn't stupid. Casual sex had never been his way.

But what was Eden expecting? He tried puzzling that out as they ate dinner. She didn't say much, though she kept sending him looks over her plate that he couldn't interpret. Nervousness? Eagerness?

Maybe a good-time girl, out for an adventure, a woman who had agreed to pose as his *bride*, for God's sake, expected something from him. His pulse began pumping, the blood pooling in his groin. What would she look like beneath that crazy dress?

She put down her fork, sending him another of those difficult-to-read looks. "I think... I think I'll turn in now."

"So—" Riley had to clear his throat. "So early? You don't want some dessert?"

Two pieces of the chef's renowned cheesecake sat on the table, each drizzled with fresh raspberry sauce. Which led Riley to thinking about Eden's taste. He focused on her mouth and she licked her lips, as if her thoughts had taken the same turn.

"Well," he said, trying to read her mind, "I hope you'll be comfortable... Make yourself right at home...."

She swallowed. "I'm sure I'll be just fine." Her tongue swiped at her lower lip again. "I just need to get out of this dress—"

Her face flushed, she broke off and then scooted away from the table. In a moment she was in the bedroom, the door shutting behind her with a quiet *snick*.

Riley drained the wine in his glass, then poured the remainder out of the bottle. His mind spun. Were her last words, her last looks an invitation? He thought again of her beautiful blue eyes, their sapphire darkness intriguing and mysterious.

This is my wedding night. His ears strained for a sound from the bedroom, and he could hear her moving around. He imagined her removing those sensible shoes, that dress, her long hair barely covering her body.

He pushed his chair back from the table. She wants me, he thought. She agreed to be my bride, didn't she? *If she wants me, I want her.*

His footsteps didn't make any sound on the thick carpeting. He focused on the bedroom door, imagining her slipping between the cool sheets, waiting for him.

He rapped lightly on the door without a prick of conscience. He'd been dumped today, *at the altar.* He deserved this good-time girl.

Her "Come in" held a tremulous note. Desire, he thought, smiling. He pushed open the door and his smile died, his excitement curdling.

She wasn't in the bed. She wasn't as he'd imagined, naked, with only her hair covering her. She didn't look the least desiring.

Or desirable.

In white again, Eden stood before the dresser mirror, a brush in her hand. A cotton nightgown covered her from chin to toes, shoulders to wrists. Though the gown was lightweight, her long hair obscured any glimpse he might have gotten of her breasts.

She looked like a woman who had never had a good time in her life.

"What is it?" she asked, sending him a nervous look.

Riley glanced over his shoulder. Surely Monty Hall must be behind him. This had all the makings of an episode of "Let's Make a Deal." And instead of finding a mouth-watering gourmet dessert behind door #1, as he'd expected, he'd found a lifetime's supply of rice pudding.

4

"This is our first test," Riley said to Eden. "Let's get going." Rolling his shoulders, he tried working out the kinks.

He hadn't gotten more than ten winks of sleep in a row all night. After backing out of the bedroom the evening before with a choked "Uh, excuse me. Never mind," he'd retreated to the living room couch. He'd spent the rest of the evening and most of the night trying to while away the hours listening to his portable cassette player.

Eyebrows raised, Eden straightened the overlapped lapels of her white terry-cloth robe with the Casa Luna logo on the breast. "Test?" Her hands fluttered to the tight knot in the sash at her waist.

"Yeah. During this poolside photo shoot we'll have to act like your average honeymoon couple." He rubbed his tired eyes. "You have your swimsuit on under there, right?"

Eden nodded. "Right. Just like you told me."

Riley nodded back. She looked apprehensive, but he tamped down his worry. Sometime in the wee hours of the morning, he'd decided that the crazy day had led him to read her signals wrong. Though Eden hadn't been coming on to him, that didn't mean she couldn't be what she'd promised—"the hottest bride a honeymoon ever had."

Still, I can't wait to get this over with. "Nervous?" he asked, and tried putting on a reassuring smile.

Her face cleared and she tossed her long hair over her shoulder. "No. I think this will be fun."

Slightly relieved, Riley chuckled. "Now that's my good-time seeker."

"That's what I said," Eden stated emphatically.

A flood of well-being washed away Riley's worry. The honeymoon would turn out okay. With Eden by his side, he had no doubt that *Getaway* would only see a happy honeymoon couple of the nineties, experiencing love—and lust—at the Casa Luna. He grinned. Eden had it right. This was gonna be fun. He slapped his palms together. "Come on, then. Let the games begin."

After shutting the door of the suite behind them, he had to hurry down the path to catch up with her. He wondered what she'd look like beneath the terry robe. Once again, most of her body was disguised and those rippling waves of hair were streaming down her back.

The lagoon pool, the Laguna Luna, had been closed for the morning to other guests. Per Miguel's orders, most of the chaise lounges had been stacked and rolled away, leaving at one corner of the pool an intimate grouping of two lounge chairs and a small table beneath a market umbrella.

Riley slung his arm across Eden's shoulders as they approached the chaise lounges. Only one other person was in sight, a groundskeeper who was meticulously sweeping up fallen hibiscus and jasmine blossoms. "Hey, Joe," Riley called out. "Where is everybody?"

The heavily suntanned man checked his watch, then looked curiously at Riley and Eden. "You're early, Mr. Smith. We didn't expect you for another twenty-five minutes. Those *Getaway* people are down at the beach, taking pictures and talking to folks."

Riley's fingers tightened on Eden's shoulders. *What was I thinking?* A groom wouldn't emerge from the bridal bed *early* on the first day of his honeymoon. He forced out a chuckle. "We're looking for food, Joe, and we couldn't wait for room service."

The groundskeeper's seamed face broke into a grin. "Ah, I understand." He winked. "And you look a little tired, too, Mr. Smith."

"Well, uh, you know." He shuffled his feet and gripped Eden against his side, just like he thought an embarrassed groom might. "Let me introduce you to my wife, Joe. This is Eden."

"Nice to meet you, Joe." Eden left his side and held out her hand to the gardener. "You do a wonderful job." She smiled that sweet smile of hers.

Joe smiled back, obviously charmed. "Why, thank you, Mrs. Smith. Arthritis is slowing me down a bit, but I guess Mr. Smith and Mr. Ortiz don't have any complaints."

"Well, they shouldn't," Eden answered emphatically. She asked him to point out some of the more unusual plants around the lagoon.

Bemused, Riley stood back and watched Eden listen intently to the old gardener. She peered at a shrub he indicated, bending over for a closer look. Riley stared at the long line of muscle in her legs, and once again thought about what was under the terry cover-up. If it was a swimsuit as charming as her manner toward Joe, they had this honeymoon thing made. *Getaway* would score some great pictures, and the Casa Luna would score some great exposure.

Riley slid his suddenly sweaty palms into the pockets of his own Casa Luna robe. To be honest, he was nervous. Very nervous. Arriving twenty-five minutes early to the photo shoot had shown him that he didn't have this honeymoon thing down yet. And if he was nervous, could he count on Eden? She didn't have a stake in this whole sham like he did.

Joe ambled off with his burlap bag and broom, and Eden came back to Riley's side. He regarded her seriously. "It's now or never, hon. In another fifteen minutes you're going to be caught forever on film as Mrs. Riley Smith. Can you do it?"

Her brow wrinkled and she crossed her arms over her chest. "How many times do I have to tell you?"

"You're a good-time girl, right? Out for an adventure."

She shuffled her feet. "Out for an adventure," she agreed.

Riley's queasy stomach settled down a bit. "We're going to pull this off, babe." His gaze slid off her face as he caught sight of someone moving along the path toward them. He groaned.

"What?" Eden asked, concern on her face. "What's the matter?"

"Miguel's mother, Margarita. I should have known she'd show up sooner or later. I'm surprised she wasn't here last night. We're in for it now."

Eden turned her head toward the tiny figure coming toward them, carrying a large tray. "Why are you so worried? She looks like a nice lady."

"Nice!" Riley groaned again. "She's a barracuda. If she doesn't sniff out the truth about us, nobody will."

Alarm registered on Eden's face. "Maybe we should just explain—"

Riley's eyes widened. "No!" He lowered his voice. "She's also got a tongue that won't quit. That woman can't keep a secret."

"Riley!" In an accented voice, the small woman called, "Are you saying bad things about me?"

He rolled his eyes toward Eden. "And she has ears like an elephant."

"I heard that," Margarita called again. "*Una elefanta,* you say. *Muchas gracias.*"

Riley shrugged. "You see?" he said to Eden, then hurried to take the tray out of Margarita's hands. "What have you here, *Mamá?*"

She smiled. "That is good. *Mamá* not *elefanta.*" She gestured toward the lounge chairs. "I have brought the breakfast. Put it down over there, *hijo.*"

Riley obeyed, setting the laden tray on the small table between the two chairs. The tray held a pitcher of orange juice, and two tall glasses filled with ice, slices of orange and sprigs of fresh mint. There were also cloth napkins and a basket of small croissants and sweet rolls. "Thank you, Margarita." He smiled at the older woman who was adjusting a gauzy scarf over her shoulders. "But shouldn't you be bringing your new designs to the clothing shop instead of bringing out food?"

Margarita smiled broadly. "And miss my first opportunity to meet your bride, *hijo?*" She turned toward Eden and held out her hand. "You should not have allowed Riley to keep you from us. But you have my best wishes."

Riley introduced the two women and watched carefully as Eden shook Margarita's hand. "Thank you. Thank you very much."

Margarita made no effort to release Eden's fingers or to hide her curiosity. She looked Eden over, from rippling hair to small sandaled feet. Her voice turned serious. "Are you happy to be his wife? Does he make your blood sing?" Margarita asked. "Does he make your heart flutter like a baby bird searching out its nest?"

The knot between Riley's shoulders tightened. If Eden couldn't fake out Margarita, they'd be in big trouble.

Eden smiled. "Your concern for Riley is admirable, ma'am. I can only answer 'Yes' to all your questions."

Margarita's intense expression didn't change. She switched her gaze to Riley. "*You* have chosen such a bride?"

Riley's guts sunk. "Wha—"

"Such a lady," Margarita went on, smiling. "You surprise me, Riley. You did very well."

Riley gulped in a deep breath. "Thank you, Margarita." He gave Eden a jubilant grin. "You hear that, babe?" *This is almost too easy.*

"Now you two, sit, sit," said Margarita. "Your bride looks like she needs something to eat, Riley. Give her a roll, pour her some juice."

Obeying the tiny woman's orders, both he and Eden settled onto the intimately grouped chaise lounges. Riley shrugged out of his robe to let the warm morning sun strike his bare chest and his legs beneath his swim trunks.

Margarita stood back, tilting her head this way and that. She then nodded. "Yes, it is good. If they take the pictures from here, the waterfall, the ocean, both will show." She paced to the end of Eden's lounge chair. "Take off your covering, too, Eden. On your young body a swimsuit will photograph better than the robe."

Riley nodded silently, agreeing. He crossed his arms and looked over at Eden with relaxed interest. They'd persuaded the staff yesterday, however briefly, that Eden was his bride. They'd managed to convince Joe, and even Margarita that they were husband and wife.

In the face of those victories, the *Getaway* folks should be a piece of cake. He checked his watch. The *Getaway* folks that should be here at any moment. He leaned back in his chair. All he had to do was sit and let those pictures snap, snap, snap. Rolls of photos of that average loving and lusty honeymoon couple of the nineties.

With slow movements, Eden untied the knot at her waist. Riley's heart started the *ka-thump, ka-thump, ka-thump*, of a car hitting speed bumps. *What was underneath there?* One shoulder rolled. Then the other. Riley's breath caught in his chest. What would a good-time gal wear? A seductive one-piece? A bikini? Maybe a *thong* bikini?

The robe slid down her arms. Eden parted the sides. And there it was.

Riley choked, that breath that was caught in his lungs trying to find a quick escape. He blinked, blinked another time. Nope, she wore the ugliest, the absolute muddiest-colored garment he'd ever seen. One-piece, with thick straps holding up a high, baggy neckline. The suit remained loose along her sides and ended in a straight, unattractive line across her thighs. It didn't look like something a bride would wear on a 1990s honeymoon. It looked like something issued to gym classes in the 1950s.

Eden bit her lip, her gaze darting from Riley's face to Margarita's. "What do you think?"

Riley choked again, then inhaled a quick breath. "We need to do something," he said, looking toward Margarita. He checked his watch. "Fast."

"I've never had much clothes sense," Eden apologized.

The only response from Margarita and Riley was the flinging of two more swimsuits over the louvered dressing room door of the resort's clothing shop.

"But are you sure this is necessary?" she asked, wriggling out of her own brown suit.

"Yes!" Margarita and Riley answered together.

Eden sighed. She didn't have much sense at all. Certainly it had taken a vacation at the same time she did. Or, more precisely, at the moment she'd met Riley Smith.

She plucked the first suit off the hanger. One piece, of part Lycra, part mesh, the white suit looked more like a one-serving pasta strainer than something that could cover, even strategically, her body.

She stepped into the leg openings, and quickly pulled it up. Then just as quickly pushed it back down. *No. No way.* She couldn't wear a swimsuit so revealing. Her naked self, for some strange reason, didn't even seem as risqué.

"Do you need some help?" Margarita's voice filtered through the louvers.

"No. No," Eden called back hastily.

She picked out another suit, this one black, with gold accents and push-up pads in the bra area. This one revealed less skin, but exposed an astonishing amount of bosom. Eden put her hand over her eyes. "How am I going to pull this off?" she whispered to herself.

Maybe she shouldn't. Maybe she'd taken this adventure idea way too far. Look what had happened! She'd agreed to be someone's—a stranger's—bride. Then she'd missed an entire night's sleep, her heart racing, her stomach in knots as her active imagination churned out fantasy after fantasy about her "groom."

She looked over the selection of other swimsuits. A bikini, way too tiny. Another swimsuit, in a cherry red color she couldn't possibly see herself in. A third bikini.

Maybe she should confess all now. She wasn't a good-time gal. She wasn't believable bride material for a man like Riley. She wasn't cut out for a honeymoon or an adventure.

"Stop your pacing, *hijo*." Margarita's voice, obviously speaking to Riley, reached Eden.

Eden strained her ears for his response. "This could do it for us, *Mamá*. If *Getaway* gives us good coverage, Miguel and I will be filling the Casa Luna's reservation book."

"I know, *hijo*," Margarita murmured. "But you are already a success with your Riley's bars."

"But the Casa Luna..." The tension in Riley's voice reached Eden's heart. "I want the Casa Luna to succeed. I *need* it to succeed."

Just like I need my adventure, Eden thought. She slipped out of the black swimsuit and wiggled back into the white one. She refused to look again at her reflection. This one would have to do.

For Riley's sake, for her own sake, she resolved again to pull this off. She was going to go through with her adventure as Riley's bride.

She caught a brief flash of her image in the mirror. Or die of embarrassment in the attempt.

Despite her resolve, Eden walked out of the dressing room with her Casa Luna robe belted tightly around her waist. "The white one," she informed Margarita and Riley.

Margarita nodded. "*Sí, sí.* I approve your choice."

Riley nodded, too. "Let's get back to the pool."

Margarita stayed behind in the shop—Riley told Eden the older woman managed the store and that many of the clothes featured were of Margarita's design—and she and Riley made it back to the Laguna Luna a full two minutes before the reporter/photographer's scheduled arrival.

Riley checked his watch. "Whew. A couple of minutes to spare. Let's get into place."

They stretched out on the lounge chairs. Again, Riley casually shrugged off his robe. Eden averted her eyes, but not quickly enough. She'd felt it before, she'd seen it once this morning, but his wide, chiseled chest and powerful shoulders set fire again to her imagination. And a washboard stomach! Now she knew the meaning of the phrase. Closing her eyes, she tried pretending she hadn't noticed.

"Take off your robe," he said.

Eden's imagination immediately detailed an entire fantasy from the suggestion. His hands at the knot of the sash. Her breath evaporating as he slowly loosened it. His fingers, each whorl on his fingertips providing its own caress, as he pushed the robe off her shoulders....

"What was the deal with that maiden-aunt swimwear?" Riley's voice intruded into her heated thoughts.

In her mind's eye, his imaginary hands fell away. She swallowed her disappointment. "I told you I don't have a lot of clothes sense."

"Are you sure this suit is any better?"

"It's fine."

"Then why won't you take off your robe?" he persisted.

Eden sighed. "Okay, okay." Obviously he wouldn't be satisfied until he saw the thing for himself.

With nervous fingers, she quickly pulled off the robe, and without meeting Riley's gaze, she fidgeted with the swimsuit, first straightening the shoulder straps, then squirming in the chaise lounge in order to inch down the high-cut leg openings.

"Stop." Riley's husky word stopped her in midsquirm. "Don't."

She lifted her head and looked at him.

"It's perfect." His gaze ran over her body. "You're perfect."

Goose bumps spread over her skin. Hot tingles that scooted across her arms and legs, and then tiptoed down her spine to pool in heated honey sensation at the small of her back. "Really?" she whispered. "You think so?"

His hand reached out and traced the line of her jaw. "I was beginning to wonder.... I have to admit I thought maybe you weren't such a good-time gal."

"I...I..."

"You turn me on," he said, his thumb stroking over her bottom lip. "You know that, don't you?"

Across her skin, another set of goose bumps tripped over the first. "I do? You...you..." She leaned into his hand and started again. "I..."

He smiled, a wealth of knowledge in his golden eyes. "Are you trying to tell me the feeling is mutual?"

She swallowed.

"Maybe we could have a good time tonight." He brushed her lower lip again, causing her mouth to part. "What do you think?"

Eden's eyes widened and she licked her suddenly dry lips, her tongue contacting his thumb. "I—"

"Sorry to interrupt, you two." Miguel's voice broke into the intimate moment. She jerked away from Riley's hand, and looked into the sun to see Riley's partner and two other people.

"I saw you coming," Riley replied, then stood, holding out his hand to the two others. "Welcome. Nadine and Eric, isn't it?"

Eden's racing heartbeat slowed. Had his gestures, his seductive talk been an act for the benefit of the *Getaway* people?

She, too, rose from her chair and shook hands with Nadine, a fiftyish pencil-thin blonde, wearing a chic sailor-accented pantsuit. Eden also shook hands with Eric, his features obscured by the brim of a baseball cap and a pair of wraparound dark glasses, his stooped figure loaded down with several cameras and other equipment.

"Sit down, sit down. We know this is really your honeymoon, you dears," said Nadine. "Just enjoy yourselves, and Eric will unobtrusively shoot his photos. I'll try to limit my questioning to Miguel."

Riley drew Eden back down to her chaise. "But don't hesitate to ask me anything you like, Nadine."

The blonde nodded, then drew Miguel away. A few feet off, Eric began setting up tripods and adjusting the lenses on his cameras.

Eden sat beside Riley in silence, listening to the murmur of voices and the gurgle-splash of the pool's waterfall. She started nervously when Riley touched her arm. "You're trembling," he said in an undertone. "Are you all right?"

"Fine, fine," she said breathlessly. A breeze blew, kicking spray from the waterfall across inches of her newly bared skin, and she swallowed. *Can I really pull this off?*

"You're sure?" Riley's brow knitted.

Eden swallowed again. "I just need something to drink."

He reached for a glass from the table between them, then frowned at the contents. "The ice is melted. Let me get you another—"

"She needs a drink with an umbrella," interjected Eric, still adjusting his camera lenses a few feet away. "Both of you do. Something icy and blended, with a pineapple spear."

Riley started to rise.

Miguel had apparently overheard. "Let me give a call to the bar," he offered, crossing to the poolside house telephone.

In two blinks, a barman delivered tall frosty glasses, filled with what appeared to be pineapple juice. Eden took a long swallow, holding a tiny umbrella-topped fruit kabob away from her lips. "Good," she said, her thirst only partially appeased. She drank again, the sweet liquid rushing down her throat. "I like this stuff."

Riley grinned. "Hold it, Mrs. Smith. Don't we need a toast?" He held up his own full glass, and they touched brims with a tiny *clink*. "To us."

The sweet liquid had changed to a warm glow of confidence that radiated from her stomach. "Mmm," she agreed. "To us." Camera shutters clicked away, but Eden didn't let the sound make her nervous. She took another swallow of her juice and smiled at Riley. "This stuff is great."

He sipped himself, then his eyes widened. "This stuff is potent."

The warm glow within her felt as delicious as the morning sun on her skin. A thought struck her. "Sunscreen." She frowned. "I'm going to have a terrible sunburn unless I put on sunscreen."

Riley's long arm scooped up a tube off the tray beside them. "Margarita thinks of everything."

Eden held out her hand. "Wonderful. Pass it to me."

He held it out of reach. "No way. This is a prerogative of the groom, you know. One of the perks of being married."

"Spreading on sunscreen?"

"You betcha." He grinned. "Turn over."

With Eric poised to record the event, Eden drained her juice, then obediently turned on the chaise lounge. Riley's hands first gathered up her hair and twisted it off to the side, then with long, sweeping strokes he smoothed the lotion down her back.

Eden sighed. The fantasy come to life! She shifted restlessly on the lounge, hoping Riley wouldn't notice the prickles of awareness racing over her skin. His palms cupped her shoulders, rubbing down to spread the sunscreen to her wrists.

He lifted his hands—she barely suppressed a protest—and then a warm line of lotion was squeezed over each of her legs. She caught her breath, and then his touch was back, large male hands massaging, smoothing, touching her like she had dreamed of the night before.

Eden's eyes drifted to half-mast, and then Eric, his khaki-clad legs anyway, walked into her line of vision. The sound of the camera clicks penetrated her haze of sensation. And she realized he was talking, as well.

"You're a lucky man."

"I think so," Riley responded.

The warm glow emanating from the pit of Eden's stomach heated up several more degrees. She *had* pulled it off. Riley's hands ran over her legs again, bumping gently into the curve of her buttocks, then sliding down to cup her heels. Eden let herself fall into a sea of sensuality.

A series of camera shutter snaps intruded again. Eden sighed in irritation. If only this Eric would go away! Then she could really bask in Riley's touch, would maybe even turn onto her back, let him massage . . .

Click click click.

Eden frowned, her fantasy again interrupted. She opened her eyes. Eric kneeled beside her, the camera lens just inches from her face.

"Sorry," he said. "I'm trying to get a different angle for the shot."

Eden shrugged, once again lowering her eyes to half-mast. She wouldn't let anything spoil her good mood, even all the pictures being taken by Eric, who'd at least stopped for a moment as he removed his wraparound sunglasses. Her adventure was turning out just right—

Oh, no.

She opened her eyes wide, and focused on Eric's now revealed face.

She knew him.

They hadn't been formally introduced, but he'd been one of two photographers sent to do the piece on the Whitney Library. What if she'd been pointed out to him? What if he knew she was Eden Whitney? *What if he calls Daddy to comment on my marriage?*

5

⟶ ⟵

"*G*etaway is going to do right by us."

Riley looked up from the paperwork on his desk into the cheerful face of his partner. "You think so, Miguel?"

The other man quietly closed the office door and leaned against it. "I know so. Nadine and Eric seem quite impressed with the Casa."

Riley pushed aside the report he'd been trying to distract himself with. "And what about Eden and me? Do you think we fooled them?"

"Fooled them?" Miguel grinned. "We could have dismantled the pool's solar panels and used you two to heat the water."

"That good, huh?" Riley rubbed a thumb against the leather corner of his desk calendar. Nothing like the silkiness of Eden's skin.

"By the way, where *is* your better half?"

Riley shook his head and shifted uncomfortably in his chair. He wished he knew. At the end of the photo shoot, just when he was hoping he could spend some private time with Eden, she'd wrapped her robe around herself like armor and scurried away. She hadn't returned to their suite. He hadn't caught sight of her on the grounds.

So he'd holed up in his office, periodically ringing their rooms, and trying not to go crazy thinking about her body in the swimsuit. After that first muddy-looking thing she'd been wearing, who could have guessed what she could do for a scrap of white Lycra?

With gritted teeth, Riley ignored the fire the mental image ignited.

"She looked damn good in that swimsuit," Miguel said, as if reading his mind.

Riley glared at him. "Do you mind? That's my wife you're talking about."

Miguel hooted. "Oh, yeah, I forgot. And how did your wedding night go?"

Riley answered with another glare. Last night's outcome was none of Miguel's business, just like what he planned for tonight was none of his partner's business, either. Judging by Eden's kitten-in-the-sun reaction to his touch, they both looked forward to that good time he'd proposed. A little food, a little wine, a long caress....

"...I knew you wouldn't object," Miguel finished.

Riley blinked. "Object? Object to what?"

Miguel frowned. "You aren't listening to me. Nadine and Eric wanted another photo shoot—in the restaurant. I said you and Eden were free for dinner."

"What?" Riley's plan included an intimate meal in their suite. "I thought Eden and I could be alone tonight."

"You're acting like this is a real honeymoon." Miguel shook his head. "Remember, Riley, this is all

so we can get that article in *Getaway.* Nadine and Eric
were ecstatic, not to mention the chef."

Riley sighed.

"Don't forget how important the exposure is for the
Casa."

Riley sighed again. "You're right, you're right." He
picked up the phone and punched in the number of the
suite. It rang. And rang. He slammed down the re-
ceiver. "What time?"

"Seven o'clock. A table on the patio, and the chef's
best dishes."

"We'll be there," Riley grumbled. So what that he
couldn't locate his bride. So what that their dinner
wouldn't be private. He'd find Eden. He'd bring her
to dinner in the Casa's dining room. He'd start their
good time under the eyes of the *Getaway* people and
after they'd said their good-night, he felt certain
they'd continue it under the sheets.

"I was worried about you this afternoon," Riley
said. "I didn't know where to find you."

Eden wrapped her arms around herself and took
another step in the direction of the restaurant, trying
to ignore the heated charm of Riley's smile. *Shouldn't
there be a law against men like this?* His nubby linen
slacks were fashioned exactly like a pair of jeans and
were paired with a pristine white silk T-shirt. He
looked like a bad boy gone good—just for the moment.

His fingers captured hers, and she started. He
smiled again. "We're honeymooners, remember?"

How could she forget? She'd made a quick exit after the morning's photo session in an attempt to re-

cover from her "groom's" intimate touch. And to figure out how disastrous was her recognition of Eric the photographer.

"So where were you?" Riley squeezed her hand.

Ribbons of sensation curled up her arm, tendrils of itchy heat that traveled beneath her oversize shirt and wrinkly broomstick skirt. Eden briefly closed her eyes, then convinced herself that she suffered from sunburn, not reaction to Riley.

She swallowed. "I was visiting with Margarita." The older woman hadn't even raised an eyebrow when Eden appeared in the resort boutique, and then stayed for ice tea after ice tea in the back room.

Riley groaned. "You didn't give anything away, did you? I told you she couldn't keep a secret."

Eden shook her head. Of course, Margarita was bound to think something about a bride abandoning her groom on their honeymoon. But she hadn't asked questions, just provided the tea, soothing chat and two aspirins. "She told me what was in that pineapple juice, you know."

"The pineapple juice?" Realization dawned across his face. "You thought that rum punch was pineapple juice?"

"Yes I did, and I gulped it like—"

"A sailor on leave."

She shot him an irritated look. "Well, thank you very much for that dainty description. You should have warned me," she grumbled. After her second glass of ice tea and waiting twenty minutes for the aspirin to kick in, she'd finally figured out why she'd gotten all oozy around Riley. It hadn't been a never-before-experienced erotic attraction at all—merely the result of warm sun, nerves and a heavily laden rum drink.

Not that Riley wasn't handsome and appealing—no woman could deny that. But she'd never actually *panted* for a man before. Never actually ached for a man's touch, and it had been a relief to rationalize— *realize* that her reaction wasn't caused by him at all.

He squeezed her hand again. "I had been hoping we could be alone for dinner. But after... We'll get to that good time, I promise."

Eden's eyes widened. No, no and *no*. She had to straighten him out. This good time stuff had gone far enough. "But, uh, Riley—"

"Shh. Here we are." He pushed open the door to a small, tropically decorated dining room. "They're waiting for us on the patio."

And they were. Miguel again, Nadine and Eric. Eden shot the photographer a wary look, but his face showed no sign of recognition at all. *Whew*. That's what she'd deduced during her ice tea and aspirin. If Eric had recognized her, surely he would have said something.

With another meaningful smile, Riley let go of her hand to lay his arm across her shoulders. Eden swallowed. Yes, her only real problem was Riley. That was the other issue she'd grappled with as she'd cooled down in the back room of the boutique.

She had to make clear to him that there was no "good time" in their future. Her thirst for an adventure didn't include hopping into bed with the first guy she ran into. She smiled humorlessly. Literally ran into.

Before they returned to the forced intimacy of their suite, she'd find a subtle way to inform him of her disinterest.

Riley removed his arm and urged her forward with his fingertips at the small of her back. Five points of erotic electricity... no, no, it was merely the sunburn again. *Disinterest,* she reminded herself.

"Sit down, dears." Nadine waved toward a table set for two. "We'll just be over here," she said, pointing to a another table. "They'll serve us the same dishes you order, so we won't even be bothering you about their taste." She smiled gaily. "With the exception of a few photographs, you'll virtually be alone!"

Terrific. Eden allowed herself to be seated. A goblet already held ice water and a lemon slice, and she took a long swallow.

Riley sat and scooted his chair toward the table, his knees bumping hers before she could draw them away. He leaned toward her. "Just relax, honey. You look like a canary being stalked by a cat."

"Tweet, tweet," she whispered to herself. If she was the feathered one, then Riley fit the image of a cat—a big cat—all smooth power and rippling muscles.

A plate of rich appetizers appeared between them. Focaccia—a cheese-topped Italian flat bread—short kabobs of grilled shrimp and cool avocado, oysters on the half shell.

Riley grinned. "Should I load up on these, babe?" he said, gesturing to the shellfish. "You know what they say about oysters."

"Riley—" Eden began.

"Perfect." The photographer moved into her line of sight and snapped a series of pictures. "Now go ahead and eat something. I promise I won't print a picture of you with crumbs on your chin."

Eden studiously avoided the oysters and picked up one of the shrimp-and-avocado kabobs. The buttery flavor of the avocado on her tongue cooled the Southwestern tang of the marinated shrimp.

Riley, of course, chose an oyster, tipping it down his throat with a quick, experienced gesture. *Click-whir, click-whir* from the camera.

Champagne was poured into waiting glasses. "Now toast each other," Eric coached. "Lean forward and look into each other's eyes."

Sighing, Eden picked up her glass and sat forward in her chair.

"Into his eyes, into his eyes," Eric urged.

She obediently lifted her lashes. And found gold. Again.

Brimming with humor and something else, something warm—no, heated—were Riley's golden eyes. "To us, baby," he said softly, and the brim of his glass touched hers at the same moment that his leg slid between her knees.

Eden gulped. Through the fabric of her skirt, the pressure and warmth of his leg against hers felt like the nudge of an unseen hand pushing her toward unknown and forbidden territory.

He smiled. "How did I get so lucky?" he whispered.

"So lucky?" she echoed faintly.

His leg began a gentle rubbing against the inside of her knee. The gauze of her skirt caressed her skin like the touch of a man's callused hand. *Tell him you're not interested.*

"I ran into you, or should I say, you ran into me?" He grinned. "Just when I needed some fun."

With a supreme effort, Eden gathered her ricocheting senses, and straightened, pulling her leg away from his. "Listen, Riley—"

"Can you do it again?" Eric's voice interrupted. "Toast one more time? I want to take it from a different angle."

Gritting her teeth, Eden obediently slid forward in her chair.

This time, Riley grabbed her free hand, entwining their fingers. He smiled. "This isn't so bad, is it?" His thumb stroked over her knuckles. "It gives us a chance to talk about tonight," he said, his voice low. "When we're alone."

The husky notes of the words crawled up her spine. When they were alone... Excitement heated her blood.

His smile curved knowingly. "We'll have that good time."

Like a dash of cold water, the words *good time* chilled her. Good time? She couldn't begin to promise Riley one. Knew she couldn't provide one even if she wanted to. She didn't have the experience necessary.

"Listen, Riley..."

"Hmm?"

Eric moved about them, pacing a circle just a few feet off, clicking away with that camera. Eden lowered her voice. "About that good time..."

"We'll make the dinner quick, I promise—"

"No, no, that's not what I mean at all," she interjected. "I just don't think we should."

"Not rush through dinner?" Riley untangled their hands and cupped her cheek. "Everyone will think it's the most natural thing in the world."

Eden gulped a swallow of her champagne. "Well, maybe I don't think it's the right thing."

Riley's brow furrowed. "What do you mean?" Then his forehead smoothed. "Are you worried about protection? I promise you I'm clean, and I have condoms—"

"No!" Eden hastened to quiet her voice, feeling the scorching heat on her cheeks. *How am I going to get through this?* These issues were almost too personal to even *think* about, let alone discuss. "I really need to be honest with you. I'm not quite the good-time gal that you think."

Riley chuckled. "I know that, hon. And to be honest with *you*, I wouldn't want to go to bed with someone that free and easy."

"Well, then," Eden said, feeling somewhat relieved.

"But I know what you do to me. What my touch does to you." He drew one long, curved finger down her cheek. "See? Goose bumps running down your neck." He leaned closer. "And your eyes are dilating. Not to worry, baby. We'll get by with the experience you *do* have."

Eden's mouth went dry. "Riley." She choked. She had to take care of this right *now*. His bad-boy aura, his confident attitude scared the pants off of her. She closed her eyes. *Oh, Eden, bad choice of words.*

She started again. "Riley—"

"Lean closer." Eric's voice came from over her left shoulder. "And, Eden, why don't you feed Riley an hors d'oeuvre?"

She blindly reached for something on the appetizer plate. A wedge of focaccia. Holding it to Riley's lips, she spoke again. "I just don't think it's a good idea. The two of us, um, *being* together." His lips opened, and she placed the bread against his tongue.

"You see, I'm not experienced at all." She took a deep breath. "As a matter of fact, I'm a virgin."

His eyes widened and he bit down. She yelped, and hastily withdrew from his mouth the fingers he'd caught in his surprise.

"Perfect!" Eric called out. "We always like to inject a little humor."

"That was a big joke, right? You being a virgin?" Riley said as soon as they were inside the door of their suite, the tense dinner over with. "And let me tell you, I'm not laughing." *Not at all,* he thought.

Eden stared at her toes. "I was serious. And what's so wrong with being a virgin, anyway? Celibacy is the in thing."

"There's nothing *wrong* with being a virgin." Riley stomped to the overstuffed chair and threw himself into it. "But it seems like someone up there is enjoying pulling poor old Riley Smith's tail."

"Oh, yeah, poor old Riley Smith." Eden took a seat on the couch, her posture straight and prim.

He groaned. "What's that supposed to mean?"

She folded her arms over her chest. "Never mind."

He stared at her; she stared back.

"So I have one last request," he said. "Would the real Eden please stand up?"

"Ha ha ha."

"Now *I'm* serious. I think you owe me an explanation."

"You require an explanation from every woman who doesn't want to go to bed with you?"

He glared. "Just the ones who go to great lengths to convince me of the good time we can have together."

She looked away. "That was just your assumption."

He wanted to throttle her pretty neck. That same neck he'd been fantasizing about as the starting point of his explorations of her body. *Groan.* "Listen, I know we had something going on between us."

An expression of remorse crossed her face. She clasped her fingers tightly together. "I just had to prove something to myself."

"At my expense?"

She blushed. "Well, maybe it seems so now, but at the time, you were asking me for a favor. You needed a bride."

"I didn't ask for a *virginal* one."

She *humphed.* "Goodness, you'd think a man would like that in the woman he was marrying."

Riley's jaw dropped. He was getting really confused here. "But we weren't getting married. I mean I know I asked—oh, hell. I'm not sure of anything except that I feel like the butt of one big cosmic joke."

"Let me clear this up for you," Eden said. "You got jilted, but you still needed a bride. You asked me to pose as your wife, and I said yes." She smiled smugly, a *see?* written all over her face.

"But you told me you could pull off the pose, no problem," he pointed out. "You said you were looking for an adventure. You said you were out for *some good times.*"

She wiggled uncomfortably on the couch. "I am looking for an adventure. That's completely true."

"And why is that?" He wanted to know the whole story. "What started you on your little quest?"

She wiggled again, but he tried not to think about her squirming hips and kept his eyes on her face. "About a month ago my supervisor had a very bad day," she said.

"Another librarian?"

She nodded.

"And?" He narrowed his eyes, determined to get it all out of her.

"She's around fifty. Long-haired, slim . . ."

"Sounds like you."

Eden nodded again, solemnly. "People have commented on it before, though we're not related. Anyway, one day I walked into her office and found her . . . weeping."

This time Riley squirmed. He hated tears. "What was she crying about?"

Eden stared at her hands. "She held a sheaf of photographs. The newest pictures of her baby niece, Sarah."

Riley snorted. "She was crying over baby pictures?"

"She was crying because the baby wasn't hers. She was crying because she'd buried herself in the library twenty-five years before and had missed out on what she saw now as the most precious parts of life."

Riley shifted in his chair, uncomfortable again. "So?" he said.

"So she looked up at me, standing in the doorway to her office. I looked back. We were both wearing beige suits. Sensible shoes. I felt like I was looking at myself twenty-five years from now. I think she felt like she was looking at herself twenty-five years ago."

Eden smoothed her long skirt over her knees. "She told me not to make the same mistakes she had. The tears were still flowing down her cheeks, falling onto those sweet pictures of the smiling baby. She said I needed to find an adventure. And a few weeks later I took her advice."

Riley snorted again. "Sounds like you don't want an adventure, sounds like you want a man."

Eden's head tilted, as if she considered his remark. "I've met 'men.' I've dated 'men.'" She pursed that mouth of hers he found so hard to ignore. "Maybe what I'm looking for is a man who makes me feel adventurous."

Panic settled like a claustrophobic cloud over Riley. That was the problem with virgins. They spoke of both "adventures" and cute pictures of pudgy babies in one breath. "Don't look at me!"

She frowned. "What's wrong with you?"

Panic again. "I'm just saying that I'm not good 'adventure' material. I'm wedding-shy, baby-shy, *virgin*-shy."

Her face pinkened again. "Would you stop talking about that? And anyway, *I* turned down *you*."

"Oh. Yeah."

She leaned back on the couch and recrossed her arms over her chest. "So if it's true-confession time, what are *you* looking for?"

"Success in business," he answered promptly. "The Riley bars are okay, but the Casa is my number one priority."

"Why is the Casa so important to you?"

He stared at her. "What do you mean?"

"I'm just thinking that you've gone to great lengths for this magazine article, for the Casa Luna itself. It must have a special meaning for you."

Yeah, it will mean that I'm more than some low-life bartender. More than some guy who came out of the slums to pour a few rounds of beer. It will mean r-e-s-p-e-c-t. "I just want to make a go of it, that's all."

"Hmm." She pursed her lips again, focusing his gaze on her mouth. He wished she'd stop doing that. "And in women... What are you looking for in a woman?"

"I'm not looking for a woman at all."

"I don't believe you," she said stubbornly. "Not a guy who nearly married yesterday."

"Hey, that experience is the basis for my comment."

She frowned. "Well, I can give you a temporary disinterest in marriage, but you must have some idea of a woman you'd like to spend time with."

"Any woman I'd consider spending time with would be..." *Not a debutante or a sweet thing.* "Would know..." *About the trashy side of life. Would know me for what I am, and wouldn't wrinkle her dainty little nose at it.* He looked at Eden, her sweet face, her dainty nose, that mouth... He refused to acknowledge the piercing pain of regret.

"You know," she said, her serious gaze on his face, "I just read a book—"

"And most of all, I want someone who hasn't depended on books for her knowledge of life." He said the words harshly, unkindly, mostly because he was reminding himself—a guy from the worst part of town, who'd left school at sixteen—of his vow. "I want a *real woman*."

6

———◆———

Eden dug her toes in the sand and savored a moment of quiet after another *Getaway* photo shoot, this one on the beach. Nadine strolled over and gestured toward Riley who was fiddling with a Jet Ski a few yards away. "So how did you and Riley meet?" she asked.

Eden curved her mouth in a practiced, carefree smile. "Oh, the usual way," she said, and turned gratefully when Eric joined them.

She surreptitiously wiped her sweaty palms against her white bathing suit while the reporter and photographer discussed their plans for the afternoon. Although she and Riley had achieved a wary truce after their discussion two nights ago, she had become increasingly tense. And through that tension, she'd still found the necessary strength to smile time and again for the *Getaway* camera.

Yesterday, she'd smiled while strolling around the beautiful grounds of the Casa Luna. Then smiled while listening to the resort's mariachi band. And now, she'd just smiled through clenched teeth while on her first-ever Jet Ski ride.

Eden sighed. She even smiled at night in her bed, thinking about the ironic fact that she couldn't sleep because she couldn't stop fantasizing about the man she refused to sleep with.

No one seemed to detect her nervousness, however. The *Getaway* people expressed satisfaction with the photos. Riley hadn't complained once about the bride-and-groom deception. Of course, he didn't speak much to her at all. In the suite, he was either discussing resort business with Miguel or plugged ever-faithfully into his portable cassette player.

Yes, apparently only Eden thought she might go mad.

She'd even begun to imagine that the photographer, Eric, was looking at her with speculative recognition.

"You need to take your bride away from the Casa."

Riley looked up from the Jet Ski he was wiping down. "What are you doing here, Margarita?" He forced a grin. "Trying to get your picture in a national magazine?"

She made a noise halfway between a *phftt* and a laugh. "Oh, *sí, sí.*" She pointed down the beach to where Nadine and Eric were chatting with Eden. "But the magazine doesn't seem interested in *me.*"

"Mmm." Riley slid his gaze off his "bride." He should go bail Eden out. Nadine had become increasingly curious about him and Eden, no matter that their relationship was really beyond the scope of her *Getaway* article. "I should go," he said to himself.

"That's right." Margarita beamed.

"That's right, what?"

"You should go, take Eden away. Spend some time, the two of you, really alone."

He frowned. "Why?"

"Men!" Margarita made another scoffing *phftt*. "Can't you see she needs to get away from the constant attention?"

Riley stared down at the grains of sand. Started counting them, to avoid admitting that exact fact. He knew Eden was becoming brittle with tension. Hell, he was a little brittle himself. But to go off *alone* with her!

The time they spent in the suite was bad enough. Any time they weren't doing the honeymoon thing for Nadine and Eric, he'd resorted to inviting Miguel back to their rooms to talk over business. They had practically planned the whole damned twenty-first century!

None of which blocked out the sound of Eden's breath, rasping across his stupidly aroused nerves in the dark, hot hours of the night.

A virgin for God's sake! A prim, librarian virgin!

But she still made him as hot as an August sun on a shadeless beach.

"Riley?"

"Yes, *Mamá?*"

"You owe her some time away."

Riley felt the cool rush of the ocean lap against his heels. "I owe her," he acknowledged. He *should* take her away today.

Yeah, maybe with some time away from the Casa and his role as the groom, he could rein in his self-destructive attraction for the totally wrong woman.

In the mirror over the bar of Riley's No. 4, Eden studied the courtship behavior of a twenty-something couple. Actually, she studied the young woman. With a flirtatious smile, the brunette drew a lingering finger down the cheek of her escort. He laughed, catching her hand and kissing it. The young woman laughed back. Dressed in a pretty sundress, the brunette seemed at ease with herself and her sexuality.

Eden sighed. If only *she* could attain what the other woman appeared to have so naturally! She slid a hand under the waistband of her black Bermuda shorts to more securely tuck in her Oxford-cloth shirt. That ease was truly what she'd been looking for on her adventure.

Problem was, how to achieve it? You couldn't just state yourself changed and let it go at that. She'd tried with Riley, and her "I'm just looking for some good times" had ended disastrously. She sighed again.

"What's the matter? Riley making you wait too long?" The Riley's No. 4 bartender, introduced to her as Stone, swiped the bar counter beside her ice tea.

"No, no," Eden replied. The longer Riley made her wait, the longer before she had to resume her role as the "bride." They'd caught a midafternoon movie, and she'd been grateful when he'd said he needed to make another stop at one of the bars he owned.

"So, what's the problem, then?" Stone asked. "Those were some big sighs."

Eden hesitated. Stone looked like a graying American gladiator, all beefy muscles and Cro-Magnon brow ridge. What would he know about a librarian who wanted to break out and be a woman? "Well..."

"Tell ol' Stone." The bartender smiled, his grin widening beneath a nose that had to have been broken once or twice. "That's part of the job description, y'know."

* * *

Riley emerged from the tiny office he kept at Riley's No. 4, the persistent problem with the ordering sheets finally straightened out.

He inhaled the distinctive, yeasty smell of beer, peanuts and good times, and rolled his shoulders. Despite nearly an hour of going over paperwork, he felt relaxed. That's what a Riley's could do for you. At least that's what Riley's had done for the knot of guys clustered at one end of the bar, if their grins and their animated discussion was any evidence.

Where's Eden? He hoped she hadn't gotten impatient and cabbed it back to the Casa. *Naah.* She'd been so thankful to get away from the resort, she wouldn't be hightailing it back there.

A smile broke across his face. The tension had eased from Eden the moment he mentioned leaving the Casa. They'd gone to the nearest multiplex movie theater, where he'd assumed she'd choose the latest artsy film and he could see the current Schwarzenegger. But surprise, surprise, the highbrow librarian had confessed to a love for action-adventure movies and they'd shared Schwarzenegger, a bucket of popcorn and a carton of Milk Duds.

The cluster of men at the bar shifted, and Riley stopped. Eden. Carrying on a serious discussion with a group of Riley regulars. He strolled forward, curious to discover what she could talk about with these guys. An informal poll on why blue collars didn't spend more time at the library? A soliloquy on the benefits of higher education?

"You think so, Hank?" Eden said, apparently oblivious to Riley's approach.

The lanky man, his badge identifying him as a worker at the nearby shipyard, nodded. "And a new hairdo."

Eden sighed. "I've heard that before."

A couple of the other men murmured agreement and then some suggestions.

"Not too short."

"But somethin' to show off your face."

Eden bit her lip. "You know, I'm sure you're right." She looked around the tight circle of men. "Thanks for the good advice."

Now just outside the group, Riley stared, dumbfounded. Eden wasn't waxing poetic on books, wasn't polling the guys as if they were a species to study. She was actually asking *their* opinion!

Her eyes, bluer than ever, shone. A little expectant smile quirked the corners of her lips.

Stone the bartender broke into the continuing hairstyle discussion. "More than a haircut, she needs someone who can show her how to cut loose. Kinda direct her breakout."

Eden's smiled died, and she nodded in agreement. "I tried doing it alone once before." Her eyes dimmed and she looked like she'd just lost her favorite kitten.

A light bulb went off in Riley's head. He forgot the tension between them and thought only of the lost beauty of her smile and that echo of excitement in her eyes. *I owe her one.*

"You need someone to help you cut loose?" He stepped forward. "I'll volunteer."

"Go away, go away." Margarita shooed Riley out of the resort's clothing boutique.

"But I want to help her pick out the dress," Riley protested.

"You gave us your suggestions, now move," Margarita insisted. "We're just going to be a few minutes, and then I'm taking her over to the salon. You may escort her to the Casa's nightclub when we are through."

The little bell on the door clanged noisily as Margarita shut it in his face. He caught one last glimpse of Eden, heading toward the dressing room with hangers over her arm.

Eden was taking the advice of the guys at the bar. "Modifying her personal style." He checked his watch. How long would it take for new clothes and new hair?

Strolling back to their honeymoon suite, he ignored a persistent, pessimistic little voice that added *and a potential whole new set of problems.*

"My little voice was right," Riley said morosely.

Disappointment waved over Eden. Was this his first and only response to three hours' worth of make-over? "I—I haven't even dared look at myself," she confessed. "Is it bad?"

Riley's face remained impassive. "See for yourself," he said. He made room for her to pass through the door of their suite. "Use the full-length mirror in the bedroom."

Eden walked slowly toward the mirror. At the salon, once a twelve-inch hank of hair had fallen to the ground, she'd firmly closed her eyes. And though she'd picked out the dress she was wearing, she had slipped into it at the salon and rushed to meet Riley before she stopped to look at the full effect of new hair, new makeup and new dress.

From the living room, Riley called to her. "I'll see you at the nightclub. We can pretend to be strangers. That way you can practice meeting and getting to know a man for the first time."

"Okay," Eden agreed, dazed. She stared at her reflection in the mirror, hardly noticing the shutting of the front door. *Is this me?*

Thank goodness she hadn't looked at herself before coming back to the suite. If she had seen the change, she didn't know if she'd have had the guts to meet Riley. "We can pretend to be strangers," he'd said. That would be easy, because she didn't recognize herself.

Her heart pounded. The white dress, a design of Margarita's, was beautiful. Of lightweight gauze, the front of the dress was modest, with a square neckline and a sleek, formfitting shape. But when she turned around—that's when her newly tanned back was bared except for two tassel-finished straps intricately twisted then slid through loops and tied at the waist.

She didn't even have to gather up her hair to expose the seven miles of bare skin. The talon-nailed hairdresser had chopped off inches of her hair—feet of it. Now the back ends tickled her shoulder blades, while the sides, highlighted to a dark gold, curved under her chin then tapered to meet the rest. Most surprising, freed from its heavy length, her hair also held a soft wave.

And then there was the makeup. That made her look different, too. Her eyes appeared darker. Her mouth almost...sultry. All this from what they'd stuffed in the tiny tote she held in her hand? A dab of mascara, the makeup woman and Margarita had said. A touch of golden eye shadow. Don't forget lipstick. "Definitely don't forget lipstick." The raspberry-colored tube was guaranteed not to kiss off.

Which made her think of Riley again. She ignored that now-familiar quiver of anticipation that feathered up her spine. He was waiting for her at the nightclub. He was waiting to help her break loose.

Once again, excitement, like the stroke of one of those tasseled straps, slid across her skin.

Eden breathed deeply. *This is it,* she thought. *If I'm ever to find the woman I can be, it will be tonight.*

On a bar stool at the crowded Casa nightclub, Riley sipped an ice-cold beer and congratulated himself again on finding an excuse to leave the suite. Hearing Eden fumbling at the door, he'd opened it to find…a goddess. A heart-pumping, shiver-me-timbers goddess.

The cut of the hair and the cut of the dress did everything that Eden's usual look didn't—it accentuated her beautiful eyes and mouth. Called attention to her gorgeous hair and small-but-curvy body. He brought his beer to his lips and swigged to keep his tongue from sticking to the roof of his mouth.

How was he going to direct her breakout, when she made his mouth go dry and his hormones go hopping?

"Hi," a throaty voice whispered in his ear. "Is this seat taken?"

The goddess had arrived. He just stared at her again, bewitched by the sight of her—her golden brown hair tickling a delicate chin, her small, but round breasts rising and falling with each breath.

"Is this seat taken?" she asked again, a nervous smile on her lips.

"No." Riley commended himself on his idea that they pretend to be strangers, though it had merely been an excuse to leave the suite. He wouldn't make a fool of himself slavering over someone he'd just met, would he?

She hitched a hip over the bar stool beside his, her movement giving him a glimpse of the sexy design of the back of her dress. *No slobbering, Smith*, he reminded himself. He'd make it through the evening by pretending they'd just met.

And by forgetting they'd go home together.

"Excuse me," he said, pitching his voice loud enough to be heard over the newly resumed music. The band had just started their next set, and couples crowded the dance floor. The nightclub had taken off in recent weeks, attracting locals as well as guests. "Can I buy you a drink?"

Her eyes opened wide and she leaned toward him. "Do I say 'yes' or 'no' when a stranger asks me that?" she stage-whispered. "This is one of those things I'm not sure about."

Riley smiled and gave a mental head shake. How could she sound so harmless, but look so like a well-packed stick of dynamite? "Well, since it's just me, just decide if you want one or not. When you're really out at a club, alone or with a woman friend, say 'yes' if the guy seems interesting to you."

She listened seriously. "Okay. That's pretty obvious. I'll have a glass of white wine, please. Thanks. And I'll buy the next round."

Riley nodded his approval. "Very good. A clear message you are your own woman. The right kind of man likes that." Suddenly an image flashed in his mind. Eden at a club, letting another man buy her drinks. *Buying another man drinks.* His palms began to sweat. "Listen, Eden, you'll be careful out there, won't you? Don't do anything rash. Don't go home with anybody. Don't let them lure you outside. Don't let—"

"*Riley.* I'm a grown woman, not a child. I won't take candy from strangers—I promise. And speaking of strangers, that's what we're supposed to be, right?"

"Yeah, right," Riley grumbled. He took a breath. "And another thing. What's that perfume you're wearing? It's too . . . seductive."

Eden rolled her eyes. "I don't believe that's the stuff of conversation between new acquaintances, or is it?"

"I'm the expert here," Riley defended. He inhaled another dose of the too-seductive perfume. To be truthful, he loved it. The scent wrapped around his libido and gave it a teasing tug, one he tried ignoring. *Strangers, remember?*

He held out his hand. "I'm Riley, by the way."

She smiled. God, he loved her mouth. "Eden. A pleasure to meet you." She gave his hand a no-nonsense shake, then picked up the wineglass in front of her and took a dainty sip.

"So what do you do for work, uh, um, Riley, isn't it?" Eden played the just-introduced well. "I'm a librarian."

"A librarian?" Riley struggled to think what he would say if he actually met a librarian in a bar. "So you spend all day helping kids with their homework and settling trivia contests?"

She drew a finger around the rim of her glass. "Well, those are a couple of the tasks of a reference librarian at a neighborhood library. But I'm the librarian for a special collection, and I also oversee the volunteer program we have. But what do you do, Riley?"

He gave her points for turning the conversation back his way. Most guys liked to talk about themselves. "I own bars and I tend bars." Of course she already knew that, but out of habit he watched her closely. This was the point where some women he'd met turned up their noses.

"Very impressive." She sounded sincere.

"Impressive?" he asked, surprised.

"What are you, thirty?"

He nodded.

"It surely took a lot of hard work and guts to get where you are."

Especially from where I came, he thought. "Yeah, well, save your awe. I also dropped out of high school." He wondered what Miss Prim Librarian would think about *that.*

Her eyes widened. "Then I'm even more impressed."

"What?"

"You've accomplished so much without many resources."

Riley blinked. *Yeah, I have.* He was astonished, though, that *she* would think so. He stared into her eyes, finding warmth, and sincerity and—

"Do you wanna dance?" An unfamiliar voice broke into the silence between them.

Riley looked over his shoulder. *Some strange guy was asking Eden to dance!* He narrowed his gaze. A good-looking strange guy. But *short,* a little voice inside him pointed out.

"You two aren't together, are you? I saw you come in alone," Shorty said to Eden.

She looked as surprised as Riley felt. Her fingers were clutching the stem of her wineglass. Her gaze darted toward Riley's. "N-no...we're not to-gether...."

"Good." Shorty held out his hand. "The band's playing a great song."

Riley couldn't believe how much he wanted Eden to refuse. But she didn't. She went ahead and let Shorty lead her out to the crowded dance floor.

Riley didn't watch. Okay, he did. Just a couple of peeks. The band rocked the room with a fast Doobie Brothers tune. Eden looked like she was having fun. Riley didn't let himself feel betrayed. Okay, he did. But just for a moment, when he saw another guy, ug-lier than the first, tug her back to the dance floor after she'd taken two steps off.

After three more dances, she finally landed back on her bar stool with a giggle.

"That was fun," she said.

Riley tried not to sound surly. "Aren't you going to dance the next one?"

She shook her head. "Not right now. I'm really not good at that fast-dance stuff. I told Bryan to ask me again when the band plays a slow one."

She was catching on to this clubbing stuff way too quickly, Riley thought. She should have spent the whole evening with him, getting indoctrinated. If she wanted to dance, especially the slow ones, she should have asked him. He was her designated stranger for the evening, damn it!

"You asked him to save you a slow one?"

Eden tucked her hair around her ears and took a sip of wine. "Uh-huh."

He shook his head, and tsked, an internal devil egging him on. "You need to be more careful, Eden." He told himself he had a valuable lesson to teach her.

"What are you talking about?" she asked him, wide-eyed.

"There's a code when you go clubbing."

"A code?" she asked, clearly puzzled.

"Yeah. There's a subtle way of expressing certain things that men and women who go clubbing understand. It's the same in other ways of meeting the opposite sex."

"'Subtle way of expressing certain things,'" she said, obviously mulling over the idea. "Maybe this is why I've never done well with men socially." Her palm slapped the bar. "I don't know the code!" She turned an astonished face his way. "So what did I say?"

Riley bit his cheek to keep a straight face. "Listen up. This is important. Asking a man to save you a slow dance is a heavy come-on," he improvised. "Kind of a 'Your place or mine?'"

Those bluer-than-blue eyes of hers became saucers. "No way!"

He nodded. "Yes way."

"No." She shook her head.

"Yes." He hissed it, because—because—because he was her designated stranger, damn it, and she should be sticking by him!

Without moving her head, she scanned the room with her eyes. "Oh, goodness, Riley, there he is, *staring* at me!" She reached out a hand to grab up her wine and take a hasty sip. "What do you think I should do? Should I just leave?"

"And have him follow you?"

She glanced frantically at him.

"No," he hastily said. "The way to cancel the come-on is to dance the next slow dance with me."

As if the band had read his mind, it segued into "When a Man Loves a Woman." Eden didn't hesitate to follow him out to the dance floor.

Any threatening attack of conscience retreated the instant he pulled her against him. One of his arms circled her—his hand against the naked, warm skin of her back. Their fingers entwined, he held his other arm straight against their sides.

Her too-seductive perfume curled around his body like insistent ribbons of desire. "Mmm." One of them made a throaty sound of satisfaction.

Riley led them around the dance floor, swaying to the bluesy voice of the lead singer. The music washed over him, and he gathered her closer. Eden snuggled willingly.

The steady drumbeat played counterpoint to the quickening pulse of his blood in his veins. His groin tightened, and he barely prevented himself from following his instincts and doing a junior high grind against her hips.

The sensuous song seemed to have gotten to Eden, too. She melted against him and buried her face against his neck. He groaned.

Her breath bathed his skin. A hot fog of desire descended on his brain. He slid his hand down her spine, letting two fingers slide beneath the waistband of her dress to caress the naked small of her back. She trembled.

What's going on here? The song seemed like more than a song, the dance more than a dance, her body more than just a body. *Why am I so turned on?* The feeling scared the hell out of him.

Thinking it had something to do with Eden's new look, he closed his eyes, then felt even more scared.

Without looking at her, his mind saw her as she was *before* the transformation—long hair, dowdy dress, colorless lipstick—and he wanted her just as much!

"Baby..." Trying to get the hoarse note out of his voice, he swallowed. "Baby, this feels so good. You feel so good."

She trembled again as he stroked her back with his two exploring fingers. "I know...." Her moving lips against his neck were like tiny teasing kisses. "Is it supposed to feel this good?"

He laughed. "I hope so." This time he couldn't stop himself from pressing his pelvis against hers.

"Mmm," she said, pushing back.

Riley shuffled them in the direction of the door. "Let's leave." He had to taste her. Touch her more.

"What?"

She sounded slightly alarmed, so Riley backed off a little. "Let's dance outside. I'm hot. Real hot."

"I'm hot, too," she complained, shifting restlessly, but making no effort to move her body away from his.

"I know," he said, and pressed a kiss against her temple. She was heat, temptation, paradise. "Let's go outside." He slid his mouth down her cheek.

She arched her neck. "We can't," she said.

In the darkest corner of the club, the one right by the back exit, Riley hesitated. "Yes, we can." He placed a kiss right below her ear.

"I don't think Bryan has seen us yet."

"What?"

"You know, the code. The one that cancels my come-on. I don't think Bryan has seen us dancing."

Riley gulped. "Oh, that."

"Mmm." She pulled his head down. "Kiss my ear again."

He let out a low laugh, a hot streak of desire shooting like a pinball through his system. "You like that?"

"Mmm."

He kissed her ear lightly. "No more until we get outside," he coaxed.

"But Bryan..."

"Honey, you've had your eyes closed practically the whole time we've been dancing. I'm sure he saw us. Let's go."

She opened her eyes now, the pupils so dilated they looked like dark moons ringed with only the faintest of mysterious blue. "But..."

Damn, I need to get her alone. I've got to touch her, kiss her.... "Honey, I made up that whole code thing," he said in desperation.

"What?"

"I made it up. I just wanted to... to..."

"*Just wanted to what?*" Her eyes suddenly became alert.

He shrugged helplessly.

Her gaze narrowed and she pulled abruptly out of his arms, her face paling. "You just wanted to make fun of my inexperience!"

She looked around wildly, then dashed through the door marked Exit, her hair and white dress fluttering like flags behind her.

7

Riley ran after her. This exit of the nightclub led to a balcony, then steps down to the moonlit sand. She had descended the stairs and was rounding a corner of the deserted beach when he caught up with her.

He gently grabbed her arm, spun her around. "That wasn't why I made that stuff up."

"Oh, yeah?" She sniffed, then stomped her foot. "'Oh, yeah?' Did you hear that? 'Oh, yeah?' You make me so crazy that the best I can do is say 'Oh, yeah?'"

He pulled her into his arms, turning his back to the lazy waves that washed onto the shore a dozen yards away. "Oh, yeah? Well, you make me crazy, too." And then he did what he'd wanted to do for days and days and hours and hours and minutes and minutes. What he'd wanted to do every damn second he'd been with her. He kissed her.

Eden moaned, her reaction to the touch of Riley's mouth overshadowing her anger. He followed the sound with his tongue, and the sheer pleasure of his invasion sent goose bumps tumbling over her skin.

He lifted his mouth. "You're cold," he said.

She simply answered, "No," and reached up for another taste of him.

His kiss was hard and possessive and set fire to, then melted, the very core of her body. She pressed herself against his wide chest and slid her tongue against the soft surface of his. *Oh, goodness, goodness.*

He left her mouth to draw in a ragged breath. She didn't think she needed air. She could live on Riley alone.

"Is this what I've been missing?" she asked him, dazed. "Why the heck did I wait so long?"

Riley's gaze narrowed. "That wasn't your first kiss."

"I've never had a kiss like *that*. No siree." She shook her head. ".I wish I'd been doing a little more dating these last few years."

He frowned and pulled her tightly against his chest. "I'll have you know that wasn't your ordinary, everyday, dating kind of kiss."

"Really?" She opened her eyes very wide.

"Really." He didn't look happy with her.

"Well, maybe I can test out your assertion. Why, I bet I could ask Bryan, or that other nice man—"

"No."

She looked at Riley innocently. "You don't think they'd kiss me? Not even on a purely experimental basis?"

Without letting her loose, he ran an impatient hand through his hair. "I can't believe you!" She kept her expression serious, but she was pleased that he seemed offended, insulted even. "You'd march in there after a kiss like we just shared and—"

"Gotcha." Her forefinger against his chest, she pulled the trigger of an imaginary pistol.

He blinked. "Gotcha?"

"Payback for your 'There's a code.'" She loved teasing him.

"Oh." A cocky grin spread across his face. "I didn't think you'd find my kisses so easy to walk away from." He lightly pecked her nose.

She smiled at him, her blood singing in her veins, her head spinning with the sheer beauty of the world, of life, of Riley. She felt wanton yet safe, thrilled yet sheltered. "Kiss me again," she demanded.

It took only the touch of his lips to turn her from smiling to sober. The way his mouth moved on hers, the way he held her so tightly, this was serious business. She needed to pay attention to it.

And she did pay attention. The heated brand of his mouth moved from her lips and slid down her neck. He bent his head to place a kiss on the hollow of her throat, and she thought she heard him murmur "Oh, yeah" through the beating wings of desire in her ears.

Now she needed air—lungfuls of it—which she tried gasping in as he explored her neck. She ran her hands over his back, kneaded the strong, male muscles of his shoulders, practically fainted when one of his hands slid from her waist to cup her breast.

The night went still. Even the waves must have paused, midcrest, because the only crashing sound she heard was that of her heart slamming against her ribs.

"Eden?" There was a question in Riley's voice.

"Yes," she whispered, no question in hers at all, because she didn't want him to stop.

His fingers squeezed gently, causing great coils of desire to spiral through her. His mouth covered her lips, and his thumb stroked across her nipple. Her hard, tight, incredibly sensitive nipple. She moaned.

His hand left her breast and she arched toward him in protest. But then she felt both hands on the exposed skin of her back, and he fumbled, briefly, until the entire top of her dress fell, baring her to the waist.

A trickle of embarrassment was quickly replaced by another surge of desire as both of Riley's hands covered her. *Aaah.* She shivered with pleasure.

"Too cold, baby?" he asked.

Cold? What could he possibly mean by cold? She shook her head, her voice completely lost. He kissed her again.

His tongue stroked hers in the same rhythm as his thumbs over her nipples. A tingling built in her body, an achy need that made her push forward against his hands and seek more of his burning kiss.

But he lifted his mouth, making her crazy again. His lips chased the goose bumps down her neck, and then moved on to kiss her breast. Hot shivers raced everywhere, before finding a home in the core of her body. His tongue licked across her nipple—*oh, my goodness*—and then his mouth took the nipple in and sucked.

Eden moaned hoarsely. She speared her fingers through his silky, dark hair and held him to her. One of his arms came around her back and arched her up to his mouth. He shifted, now suckling the other breast.

Dark, electric pulses of need ran on hot pathways to her womb. She pulled Riley's shirt from his waistband and slid her hand over the skin of his belly, then his chest. He groaned, the sound urging her on until she found his light fur, the tight point of one of his nipples.

"Eden..." He kissed her again, his mouth opening hers wide, his tongue somehow knowing how to match the rhythm of that primitive pulse beat in her body. One of his hands stroked her breast again.

Air breezed across her legs. Her naked legs. Riley's other hand had inched up her skirt. He laid his palm, hot and knowing, over her panties, over the very heart of her. He pressed, his hand rocking with that same rhythm. She writhed against him.

"Riley?" She said into his mouth. Where the heel of his hand massaged her body, another shot of fire streaked through her. She lifted her mouth. "Riley?"

He looked down at her, the moonlight in his eyes, silvering their gold. "Feel it, Eden." He bent his head to lightly suck her neck. "Feel it."

The tingling had built into a pyramid of need that he made her climb. Every rhythmic move of his hand, every wet caress of his mouth, urged her higher.

He accelerated the rhythm, making her climb faster now. His lips found hers again, his other hand stroked and teased her nipples. *One more step to go.* She didn't know where to, exactly, she just knew one more step.

He must have known how close she was, too. Riley released her mouth, then lowered his head to her breast. He wet a nipple with his tongue. She shuddered. *Just a half step more.* He wet the nipple again, then took it in, sucking, while the heel of his hand pressed strongly against her body, coaxing her that last half step. Coaxing her . . . *there.*

No sounds again. No smells, no taste, nothing but waves of incredible rocking pleasure and the silver of the moon and the gold of Riley's eyes.

He held her in his arms while the pleasure ebbed away, leaving behind delight that shivered her at increasingly long intervals.

Finally returned to earth, she ran her tongue over her lips, and felt each of the buttons on his shirt against the bare skin of her chest. She swallowed. *What did one do now?*

The silence stretched out. "I...um... Thank you." She kept her head buried against him. "Should I say thank you?"

He chuckled, a warm rumble against her cheek. "If you want to."

She licked her lips again, still embarrassed, but itching to say more. "That was it, wasn't it? Not *it* it, but it."

He laughed again. "That was one of the most important parts of *it.*"

"But I've really had one of *those,* now, right?" She blinked at the great wonder of it. "You know, some women go their whole lives without one of *those.*"

He rubbed her head in an affectionate gesture. "You definitely had one of *those.* As a matter of fact, it's incredible how easily you have one of *those.*"

She bit her lip. There was more to be said here, but it was tough going. "Uh, Riley?"

"Hmm?" He rested his chin against the top of her head and stroked her back. Another affectionate gesture. It had none of the passion and sensuality of his earlier caresses.

"Um, well, *you.*" She swallowed again. "Shouldn't we do *it* or something so that you have one of *those?*" She snuggled closer against him. The idea of pleasing Riley, of making him feel what she had, rekindled a warm glow in her belly. "Wouldn't that be a good idea?"

"No," he said, his voice rough, his body suddenly tense. "I don't think that would be a good idea at all."

Back in their suite, her dress having been hastily re-tied before their silent return, Eden gathered up her courage. She needed to know why he thought doing *it* with her would be a bad idea. Swinging around, she confronted a stony-faced Riley. "Explain yourself."

"I told you," he said stubbornly. "I don't want to talk about it."

"Well, I do!"

He rolled his eyes. "And to think, I once thought you were the silent type."

"Help me out here, Riley." She dropped onto the soft couch. "This situation is awkward for me."

He shoved his hand in his pocket and came out with a velvet, ring-size jeweler's box. "Then let's not talk about it anymore." He turned the box over and over in his hands.

"We haven't talked about it at all!"

He sighed. "Listen, Eden. I'll admit you turn me on. I *vroom* to life like a Ferrari when you touch me, when you look at me, if you want to know the truth. But that doesn't mean we're gonna have sex."

A wave of heat crept up Eden's face. "But...but..." Should she feel flattered by his admission or insulted by his disinterest in having her in his bed?

"But what?" He kept his gaze focused on that little box.

"I guess I just feel a little...selfish."

"You don't owe anybody sex," he said harshly. "And don't you ever forget that!"

"Of course not," Eden answered. But if she wanted to share her body with him, wanted to share with him the incredible pleasure—

"We're not right together, damn it!"

She looked up, startled by the anger in his voice.

"Not right at all!" He walked out the front door of the suite and slammed it shut.

Eden looked after him in confusion and dismay. It took her a little while to understand what he'd been trying to say, though it shouldn't have. Hadn't he told her time and again that he needed a "real woman"?

What Riley hadn't wanted to discuss, what she had tried forcing out of him, was that while he might find her attractive, she just wasn't enough woman for him.

With a sigh that had a suspicious hiccup in it, she walked into the bedroom. She wasn't going to cry. No, she could do all that another time, when she didn't need to look like a cheerful honeymooner in the morning. Because if Riley didn't want her in his bed, the least she could do was be the happiest-looking gosh-darn bride in the universe.

The door to his office opened, then shut with a bang. Riley groaned, but refused to open his eyes. His desk chair was a hell of a spot to get a good night's rest, and he was sure he'd only just fallen asleep.

"It's 9:00 a.m.," said his partner's voice.

"Thank you, Mr. Town Crier."

"I've been looking for you everywhere."

"You found me," Riley grumbled. "So what did you want?"

"Nadine and Eric are leaving today."

Riley's eyes popped open. He'd thought those two were staying until tomorrow, maybe the day after. "What did you say?"

"They're leaving today. They're ecstatic with the material they have, and they want to get back and work on the article."

Finally, some good luck! That meant Eden could leave today, too! He'd not have to spend even one more day being tortured by her scent, her touch, by the fantasies of what they *could* have been doing last night.

"Eden didn't know where you were," Miguel said disapprovingly. "Is that any way to treat your wife?"

Riley rubbed his aching head. "You know she's not my wife. Never could be. Never will be. You know I've sworn off commitment."

That was what had stopped him last night. When she'd responded so willingly, so sweetly to his touch, when she'd come apart in his arms, he'd realized he couldn't take her to bed. They were people from two different worlds, and not only did she deserve more than he was, she deserved more than he was able to give.

He picked up the ring box from where it lay on his desk and snapped it open. The platinum band winked in the morning sunshine, a dot-dot-dash of light, a kind of Morse code for "You did the right thing."

"So when are they taking off?" he asked Miguel. "I'll be there with bells on to wave Nadine and Eric goodbye."

"This afternoon, sometime. After the last photo shoot." Miguel smiled smugly.

A chill rushed down Riley's back. "What last photo shoot?"

"The last photo shoot of the honeymoon couple." Miguel's smile widened. "In bed."

Eden didn't ask Riley where he'd spent the night. She couldn't have even if she wanted to. The minute he'd returned to the suite, shortly after Miguel had come looking for him, he'd clapped his ever-present headphones over his ears and switched on his portable cassette player. He sat morosely on the couch, his fidgety legs indicating he was listening to more rock 'n' roll.

She stared at the back of his dark head, trying to feel relieved. When Miguel had told her about the last photo shoot, an overwhelming feeling of doom had slid over her. Without Riley, how would she pull off the last man-and-wife deception?

But the doom and gloom hadn't lifted with Riley's reappearance. Maybe it was just more nerves, or lack of sleep, but *something* was unsettled inside her. Something to do with Riley. Something she couldn't quite put her finger on.

"What are you doing?" His voice penetrated her thoughts.

She looked down at the throw pillow she'd been absently kneading. "Fluffing." She tossed the pillow on the overstuffed chair. "I want everything just perfect for the last pictures."

He grunted, and settled the headphones back on his ears. "We're going to another suite for the shoot. Eric's setting up all his equipment there so he wouldn't be in our way." He paused. "They think they'll make one of these photos the cover."

Another wave of nervousness washed over Eden. "Really?"

"Really." The cassette player switched back on with an audible click.

Sighing, Eden headed for the bedroom. If the photo shoot wasn't going to be in their room, she could get out her suitcase and start packing.

Another click of the cassette player. "I'm sorry," Riley said.

She paused, looking over her shoulder. "Sorry?"

He gestured vaguely. "I'm sorry I got you involved in all this."

"That's okay."

He frowned. "I want you to know this wasn't all just for me."

"Oh?" She felt a bite of disappointment. For some strange reason, she wanted it to be just for him.

"Miguel...Margarita..." He pushed the headphones off his ears so they hung around his neck. "Miguel has been my accountant for the last four years. He wanted to invest in something with me...become equal partners in a new venture."

"And you were nice enough to let him join you in the Casa Luna."

"No." He frowned again. "That's not what I mean at all. Miguel had to convince me that we—that *I*—could pull off a classy business like a honeymoon hotel. It took him a while, but he finally did. All his savings are tied up here. Margarita's, too, as well as her pride in her clothes design business."

"You didn't want to let them down."

"I couldn't. Don't you see? This spread in *Getaway* is going to do it for us. The success of the Casa is going to prove something to Miguel and Margarita."

"And to you?" she prompted quietly.

His hand slid in his pocket and he pulled out that velvet jeweler's box again. He rolled it between his fingers. "Yeah. Maybe."

A silence welled between them, but she didn't think he noticed.

"Maybe it will prove that they were wrong about me," he murmured.

Something told her not to ask him what he meant. And as if he hadn't realized he'd even spoken aloud, he placed the headphones back on his head and turned on the player.

Eden walked into the bedroom and began packing, mulling over what he'd said. *Prove wrong about what to whom?* She'd probably never find out. A flock of drunken butterflies took off in her stomach. After today, she'd probably never see Riley again. *Why does that make me feel queasy?*

Click. From behind her, the cassette player turned off again. She turned her head to find him lounging against the doorway, watching her.

"What are you going to wear for the shoot?" he asked.

Her eyes widened. "I don't know.... I hadn't thought.... What do they want me to wear?"

He shrugged. "I don't know, either."

From the bed, she picked up her flannel nightgown. "This?" She held it up.

They both shook their heads. "No," they said together.

She bit her lip and ruffled through the clothes she'd already placed in the suitcase. "Um...um..." She frowned, then brightened, inspired. "What if I wear nothing?"

"Wear nothing?" he repeated, his face as astonished as if she'd said wear nutshells.

"Yes. Eric wouldn't have to see anything." She placed her hand on the flat part of her chest. "It would be just you and me under the covers, and if we kept the sheet up to here—"

"*No.*" Riley's voice was hoarse. "God, *no.*" He started talking very fast, almost babbling. "Not a good idea. I wouldn't live...I mean I wouldn't like...I mean..." He took a breath. "Just *no.*"

He disappeared from the doorway and showed up a second later. "Wear this," he said, tossing something at her. "And button it all the way up."

"O-okay." Boy, was he agitated. "You're sure it wouldn't be better if I was na—"

"Don't say it." He held up his hand. "I've got to get out of here," he mumbled, plucking the headphones from around his neck and throwing them and the cassette player onto the bed. "Think something cold. Ice. Think ice."

She frowned. "Ice? What are you talking about?"

"I'm talking about the photo shoot, the bed, you being naked." He slapped his palm against his forehead. "Don't think about that, Smith. Ice. Think ice." He groaned. "Oh, God, I feel a disaster coming on."

She didn't like Riley voicing doubts. "You don't think we can pull it off?" she asked, her own nervousness redoubling.

Riley just stared at her stupidly. "Don't talk about pulling anything off, okay? Don't talk about being naked or pulling anything off. I gotta go. Ice." Catching her befuddled look, he explained hastily. "Maybe they need some. For some reason I know I do." He dashed out of the suite, calling over his shoulder. "I'll meet you in Suite 2223 in an hour."

Eden stared after Riley. An hour until the photo shoot. Their last photo shoot. Their last time together pretending to be honeymooners.

She held up the garment he'd thrown at her, the one to wear for the shoot. His tuxedo shirt. She rubbed its tiny pleats against her cheek. The shirt smelled good—warm, male, exciting. Like Riley.

That queasiness took over her stomach again. More gloom and doom that caused her heart to thud ominously. *What's wrong with me? Surely we can make Eric and Nadine believe one more time.*

But this time when she thought about the deception, she realized that wasn't what had been bothering her after all. It was what came after the photo shoot. Because after it was over, she'd be leaving Riley.

The butterflies started another wild flight. *Thud. Thud. Thud.* Her heart beat a funereal dirge against her ribs.

To avoid the sound and what it might mean, she grabbed Riley's headset and cassette player off the bed. She'd distract herself with a little music. Let the raucous beat of rock 'n' roll drown out her thoughts, her feelings....

Headphones over her ears, she flicked on the player, bracing herself for a loud blast of music. A tinny hiss, then: "Call me Ishmael."

The voice of the narrator droned on, but Eden didn't listen. "Call me Ishmael"? The famous, infamous, first sentence of the first chapter of Herman Melville's *Moby Dick*. Riley was listening to *Moby Dick?* No. Maybe an alternative rock group used the distinct line. With her fingernail, she flipped open the cassette player and stared down at the label on the tape. "The Unabridged Classics, Volume XXVII, *Moby Dick* by Herman Melville."

Not a rock group, but Melville himself. Unabridged!

If she remembered correctly, they made you read it in high school—Senior English. Gad, nobody *elected* to read an unabridged edition of *Moby Dick*.

Unless somebody hadn't taken Senior English. She suddenly remembered Riley telling her he hadn't finished high school. Unless somebody hadn't taken Senior English but instead had dropped out and gone on to start a series of successful businesses, yet still felt like he wasn't good enough. Like he had to prove something.

Eden stared down at the tape player. It didn't take a genius to figure out that all those times she thought Riley had been plugged into rock 'n' roll, he'd really been plugged into the classics, *unabridged,* somewhere between volumes one through twenty-seven.

What a fascinating man he is.

Thud, thud, thud. Her heart double-timed. The flock of butterflies took another tour of her stomach. Familiar feelings of uneasiness, queasiness and doom rose up and then flattened out as understanding dawned.

She loved him.

She loved Riley, the man of ceaseless contradictions. The thrilling man who could seduce her with a smile, yet with whom she always felt safe. The man who'd succeeded on his own, yet who wanted another success for Miguel and Margarita. The man of cocky confidence who was still trying to measure up to some internal standard.

Oh, God, she really, really loved him.

What am I going to do now?

Never having loved before, she was at a complete loss.

She took a deep breath. Another. Suddenly the suite felt too confining. For some reason, acknowledging her love seemed to allow her feelings to grow stronger and stronger with each lungful of oxygen. With shaking hands, she dropped the tuxedo shirt and the cassette player back on the bed.

She had to find more space.

Opening the door, she bumped into Margarita, the other woman's hand raised as if ready to knock. Eden barely avoided a rap on the nose. "Margarita!"

"*Sí, sí.* And you are just the woman I wanted to visit." Margarita bustled past Eden into the too-small suite. "Come and talk to me." She stationed herself on the couch and patted the cushion beside her.

Eden swallowed. She couldn't ignore Margarita's request, but she didn't feel capable of any small talk right now. She was afraid she'd blurt out "I love him!" any second.

"Come, come," the other woman urged.

Eden shuffled on slow-moving feet to the couch and took the prescribed seat.

"So, how are you?" Margarita asked, a gentle smile on her face.

Eden tried smiling back. "I love him!" she blurted out, then burst into tears.

The next few minutes passed in watery confusion. Margarita's "I know, I know," seemed to cover all the points of the story that Eden was stammering out between dabs of tissue.

Eden dried her eyes again and lifted her head. "You know we are just pretending to be married?"

"*Sí.*"

"You know that I love him?"

"*Sí.*"

"So what should I do about this whole mess?"

Margarita smiled and patted her shoulder. "Now *that* I do not know."

Eden groaned. "I'm in terrible trouble."

Margarita laughed. "You are in the trouble of all women all over the world."

"All women? All over the world?"

Margarita nodded her dark head. "At one time or another, each woman must struggle with how to make her man realize he cannot live without her."

Eden opened her mouth to protest that in the nineties it wasn't so simple, so gender-based. But Margarita's words matched Eden's own experience so she merely shrugged. "At least I'm in good company."

They sat together in womanly companionship. Finally Eden sighed. "So when did you figure out the honeymoon was a sham?"

Margarita smiled sympathetically. "From the first. Although I'd not met Riley's fiancée, I'd seen her picture. You look nothing like her."

Eden grimaced. "Please. Don't rub it in."

Margarita laughed. "It is not what you are thinking. She is a platinum blonde, you see."

Eden rolled her eyes. "Very clearly, I assure you." Platinum blonde, 36D, legs up to her armpits. Ugh. Even the imagined image of such a "real woman" made her want to pack her suitcase and sneak out the back door. "But I still have the last photo shoot," she murmured to herself.

"What is that?"

"Oh, nothing. I was just thinking about the pictures they're going to take of Riley and me. They want to get a photo of us in bed for the cover of *Getaway*." She forced on a smile. "Then I'll be on my way."

One of Margarita's fuchsia-tipped fingernails tapped her chin. "In bed?"

"Mmm."

"What are you planning on wearing?"

"At Riley's order, his tuxedo shirt, buttoned to the chin."

"Oh, this is good. Very good." Margarita smiled. "Buttoned to the chin, he ordered?" She rubbed her palms together. "What do you say to a small wardrobe change?" She laughed. "Very, very small."

"A wardrobe change?" The crafty expression on Margarita's face gave Eden hope. "I have no objection at all. What do you have in mind?"

Margarita stood, then pulled Eden up by the hand. "Come along with me. My boutique is not in a honeymoon hotel for nothing."

* * *

Riley decided the in-bed photo shoot would be a snap. No sweat. What with all the tripods, lights and other paraphernalia set up around the bed, there wasn't a chance that it would feel the least bit intimate.

He grinned in Miguel's direction. "Hey, partner, I'm almost an unmarried man again. A few clicks of the shutter and this will all be just a bad dream."

"Shh." Miguel shot a look toward the suite's front door. "Eric will be back any minute."

"Relax." Riley plopped on the mattress and crossed his legs. "This is gonna be easy, even if I am wearing these goofy pajama bottoms."

"Hey, they're from the Casa boutique and you certainly couldn't wear your usual—nothing."

Riley stared down at the loose-fitting pants. The white cotton had a stripe the same blue as Eden's eyes. Paradise blue. He shook off the thought.

"Yeah," he said heartily. He crossed his arms behind his head. "Eden'll come in, snap snap will go the pix, we kiss ol' Eric and Nadine goodbye, then I get the quickiest divorce on record."

"And then your bride conveniently rides off into the sunset?"

Riley frowned at the sarcastic edge to Miguel's voice. "What's wrong with you? You were for this honeymoon as much as I was."

"And I'm feeling bad about it. I like Eden. She's a nice woman."

"Well, then you marry her." Riley immediately regretted the flip response. He sat up and stared his partner in the eye. "I'm kidding, you know. Hands off Eden."

Miguel shrugged. "Hey, if you're 'divorced,' I don't know what you have to say about the matter."

"I have everything to say about it." Riley found himself on the soles of his bare feet, pacing toward his partner. "You understand?"

Miguel's hands shot up, palms out. "Take it easy, Riley. I'm not after your woman."

Riley walked back to the bed. "She's not my woman," he grumbled.

Miguel's eyebrows rose. "You're a nut case, you know that?"

"I'm just setting the record straight."

"Well, I'm setting the record straight right back at you. You've got a thing for that woman."

"She's a librarian," Riley explained.

Miguel shrugged. "And you're a businessman."

"I'm a *bartender.*"

"I give up." Miguel shook his head. "I can't win."

"You got that right." Nothing could convince Riley to act on his "thing" for Eden. And yeah, he did have one for her, for some kooky reason, but she was the wrong woman for him. He was definitely the wrong man for her. *She's going to leave the Casa Luna as untouched as when she arrived.* He blinked away the blazing image of those long minutes with her on the beach.

Don't touch her again, Smith.

Unfortunately, the photographer had other ideas. When Eden showed up in the suite, the guy waxed poetic on her new hair and makeup. And when she unbelted her Casa Luna terry robe to reveal the tux-

edo shirt that covered her from kneecaps to neck, Eric
thought a photo of Riley tossing Eden onto the bed
would make a "hot shot."

So, to hurry things along, Riley swallowed his protest and took Eden up in his arms. She was light as sea-
foam, and that seductive perfume of hers curled as
naturally up to his nose as her arms did around his
neck. He refused to meet Miguel's eyes, who slipped
out of the suite wearing a knowing smile.

"Feel silly?" Riley asked, slanting a look at her as
they waited for Eric to finish fussing with his cameras
and give the go-ahead.

"Not silly at all." She smiled, a knowing woman-
smile, that was like a tantalizing fingernail down his
spine.

"Well, you, uh, look great," he said, shifting uncomfortably from foot to foot.

"Thanks." She reached up to kiss his chin, and as
her lips pressed softly, her tongue stole out and stroked
him wetly.

Stunned, he dropped her on the mattress.

"Hey, I wasn't ready!" Eric protested. "You're
going to have to pick her up again."

Riley gave Eden a stern look. "See what you made
me do?" As he pulled her back into his arms, she
murmured something. "What did you say?"

She whispered into his ear. "I said, *I'm* ready." She
smiled again, that smile like a fingernail tickle.

Oh, God. An all-too-familiar tightening in his groin
signaled problems. Real problems. He mentally
thanked Eric for the sissy pajama bottoms. The
drawstring style was full enough to cover the worst of
his reaction to Eden's teasing words.

"Behave," he said, a warning in his look.

"And if I don't?" She smiled saucily, determination shining in her eyes.

When Eric said "Drop" Riley couldn't comply quick enough.

If only that was the end of the torture, Riley thought a few minutes later. But no, now Eric wanted them *between* the sheets, and apparently the photographer was practicing for his Hollywood directorial debut. "Sultry," the man called out. "Think wedding night." He'd positioned them on opposite pillows, not touching, thank God, their cheeks turned so they faced one another in profile.

Eric stepped onto the bed and took an instant shot "to assess the picture's composition." Then he cautioned them against moving a muscle. "Blink and breathe. That's it."

Riley stared at Eden. "You don't look so good. Are you feeling faint or something?"

Her eyebrows came together. "I was thinking wedding night. You know. *Sultry.*"

"I hate to break it to you, doll, but you look sick, not sultry." It was a whopping lie. But he had to say something to distract him from her flushed cheeks, from her mouth that looked soft and wet and ready to be kissed.

"Is that so?" Her gaze narrowed. "Well, you look kind of... bothered. Yes. *Hot* and bothered."

"Me?" His voice had an annoying hoarseness to it. "I'm as cool as a cucumber. Why, I'm just counting the minutes until this is over."

"Really?" She didn't look like she believed him. "Cool as a cucumber?"

Then he felt it. A short stroke on his ankle. The touch of warm bare flesh against his warm bare flesh. "What the hell are you doing?"

Her eyes rounded innocently. "What are you talking about?"

"I feel something on my leg. It's either a bedbug or it's you."

She giggled. "Oh, *that*. It's just my toe."

"Just her toe" started playing hopscotch up his shin, dragging back the hem of his pajamas with each teasing movement. "Don't do that." A trickle of sweat rolled down his back.

She inched her face closer and pinned him with her gaze. "Why not, Mr. Cool?" she whispered.

"Perfect!" A camera shutter clicked in quick succession. "Sultry as a steam bath," Eric called. "Great job, you two. You can relax for a couple of minutes."

Riley swiftly rolled out of bed and dashed to help himself to a glass of ice water from the tray on the dressing table. In the mirror he caught sight of Eden across the room in low-voiced conversation with Eric.

Another bead of sweat formed at his nape. "Let's get moving, okay? How many more of these do you really need, Eric?"

The other man grinned at Eden then looked his way. "Not too much longer. But I have a few more ideas I want to try out."

"A few more ideas?" Riley frowned. "Come on, haven't you got plenty of our mug shots?"

"Get back in the bed, if you would," Eric answered noncommittally. "Eden, snuggle up next to him."

With the pillows plumped, Riley propped himself against the bed's headboard, and Eden obediently settled herself in the crook of his arm. Eric took a few pictures, frowning all the while. Riley frowned, too, trying to ignore the sweet scent and sweet feel of Eden in his arms.

"Eden, turn over, would you?" Eric directed. "Put an arm on either side of Riley as if you're about to lower yourself to kiss him."

In a flash Riley was imprisoned by Eden's arms. She held her body away from him, though he could feel the heated imprint of her leg against one of his pajama-clad ones. A lock of her shortened hair fell forward, its length now unable to reach his bare chest. *Damn haircut.*

Her minty breath bathed his face. He focused on the fresh scent so he'd forget about her beautiful features above him, so he'd forget about how her mouth and breasts hovered over him. "Crest? Pepsodent? Mentadent?" he asked flippantly. "Remind me to use your toothpaste next time."

She shook her head slightly. "There isn't going to be a next time," she murmured, for his ears only. "My toothbrush and toothpaste are all packed up, Riley."

"Don't talk about that," he said, irritated by the reminder.

"Because you don't want Eric to hear?"

"Yeah. What is that fool doing anyway?" Riley craned his neck to see over Eden's shoulder. He spied the man rummaging through a bag in the corner of the bedroom. "What's the holdup, Eric?" he called out.

The other man ignored him.

"I'm in no hurry," Eden said. "I could look at you all day." She lowered herself to her elbows.

Riley groaned as the weight of her breasts beneath the tuxedo shirt settled against his chest. "Don't talk like that."

"Why?"

"Because..." Riley gulped as she wiggled, settling herself more fully against him. "Because..."

"Because for some reason you don't want me to know you."

"What are you talking about?" Riley couldn't think. His little voice reminded him of his vow to leave her untouched even as one of his hands came around to stroke the small of her back. "I don't know what you mean." Her heartbeat pounded against his chest.

"I put your headphones on. I listened to your tape."

"Mmm." He listened to both their heartbeats, a dual thrumming in his ears that drowned out the cautions of his inner voice.

"Moby Dick?" One of her fingers traced the line of his eyebrow and he felt the stroke like a feather's touch across his entire body. "You didn't tell me you were listening to the classics."

"Catching up on the classics." This time her finger moved across his eyebrow to draw a line down his cheek, and he made himself ignore the tender touch. "I read them, too, but the tapes are more convenient. I can listen in the car, in the office—" He caught his breath as her finger traced his ear. He grabbed her hand, but gathered her closer with his arm around her waist. "Eden—"

"Show time, girls and boys!" Eric called.

Riley came to his senses and sat up straighter, pushing Eden gently away from him. "This is *it*, Eric. A couple more pictures and then we're through." He didn't look at Eden.

Eric grinned. "Hey, I catch your drift. Just a few more. Can you get back into position?"

With a resigned sigh, Riley slid back down on the pillows. Again, Eden placed an arm on either side of him. He still didn't look her in the face.

"Now I love this tuxedo shirt idea, guys," Eric said. "But can we loosen it up a little? Riley, undo the first button."

Groan. The last thing Riley should be doing was unbuttoning Eden. But his fingers reached up and fumbled with the top button for long seconds. He finally got it open, to reveal the entrancing hollow of her throat. Fascinated, he watched her pulse beat frantically against her skin. "Nervous?" he said, making the mistake of looking at her.

"Yes," she whispered. Her open gaze met his. "Very nervous."

"Unbutton another," Eric called out.

Riley's fingers obeyed. In the background, he heard the clicking of the camera. His unbuttoning revealed a small vee of Eden's smooth, fragrant skin.

"Another," said Eric.

Riley heard Eden's breathing, watched the pleats of the tuxedo shirt rise and fall. "No way," he said flatly. "Not with Eric here."

"I have something on underneath," she said. "I told Eric."

"What are you talking about?"

Eden pulled away and sat up, on her knees. "I have something on underneath the shirt, something I thought might look better in the photograph than the shirt." As Riley's jaw dropped, her fingers swiftly unfastened the remaining buttons.

"See?" she said, shrugging off the white shirt.

Riley's eyes widened. He saw, all right. A peach-colored, lace...*something* that covered everything and nothing. Something that belonged in a lingerie catalog, not on the woman he—well, not on Eden, and especially not with Eric looking on!

In a move better suited for a football game than a photo shoot, Riley tackled Eden, pushing her back across the pillows and covering her body with his to shield her from Eric and his camera lens. "Good God, Eden..." He lay over her, the feel of warm lace against his skin an aphrodisiac to tempt the best intentioned of men.

"'Good God, Eden,' what?" Her expression showed delight instead of surprise. She framed his face with her hands. "I love—" She took a breath. "I love the way you feel against me."

And what could a man say to that? Riley thought. It didn't seem a moment for words. As a matter of fact, when it came to Eden, he was sick to death of words. Sick to death of his little voice's warnings.

He kissed her, his mouth open, hot, wanting.

And from the fuzzy edges of Riley's mind, right before he heard the front door of the suite open and close leaving the two of them alone, Eric called, in the best Hollywood style, "That's a wrap!"

Riley's kiss ended much too soon. Eden stared at him when he lifted his head. "We're getting out of here," he said brusquely.

"But—but—" They were finally alone, and now he wanted to leave? Apparently Margarita was wrong that Riley only needed a little push to realize he couldn't live without her.

He rolled off her, then rolled off the bed, his warmth replaced by chills across her skin. He grabbed up the terry robe she'd arrived in and tossed it over her. "Put this on."

Riley turned his back while she struggled into the sleeves. What a disaster! A hot wash of humiliation rose up her neck. He couldn't have missed her so-obvious, and apparently so-useless, attempts at seduction. A prick of tears stung her eyes as he grabbed her hand and marched her out of the suite.

Fallen hibiscus blossoms crushed beneath his heavy steps as he led the way back to their room. *He can't get rid of me fast enough,* she thought. She blinked rapidly to dispel the excess moisture from her eyes.

The door to their suite opened, then shut with a clunking goodbye knell. Riley let go of her hand, and she leaned against the back of the door, uncertain of what to say or do. So long? It's been fun? *I'm in love with you?*

He stood staring at her, his gaze unreadable, his arms folded across his bare chest. She realized he'd walked through the public grounds of the Casa Luna in pajama bottoms. She giggled, a nervous titter. Only Riley, her attitude man, could pull that off.

"What are you laughing at?" His eyes narrowed.

She gestured vaguely. "Your awning-striped pj's."

He frowned. "You shouldn't be one to talk about pj's. Where the hell did you get that lace thing?"

Eden felt herself flush. "Margarita. There's a whole lingerie section in the boutique."

He shook his head. "You shouldn't have put it on."

"It looked that bad?" Eden bit her lip. She'd wanted to be a hot, "real woman," for him. Obviously the librarian in her just couldn't pull it off.

"I don't like Eric seeing you like that."

"That ridiculous?"

He shot her a puzzled glance. "It shows too much skin."

Eden frowned. "It covers more than my bathing suit!"

He just shook his head stubbornly. "I don't like him seeing you like that."

Eden flattened her palms against the door and pushed away. "Well, since it's all over, I guess there's no more worry of that." She turned her shoulder to move past him.

His fingers grabbed her upper arm. "Where do you think you're going?"

Surprised, she looked up. "To the bedroom, to finish..."

"What we started?" he suggested quietly, then his mouth sank down, possessively, on hers.

Eden's head spun. His lips burned passionate heat, his tongue only slightly cooling her mouth as it licked her lower lip. Then he broke off the kiss and stared at her again, leaving Eden panting and confused.

"W-was that goodbye?" she asked.

"Goodbye?" He blinked. "Hell, Eden, did that taste like goodbye?"

She backed out of his arms. "No. Yes. But you said.... I'm so confused." She rubbed at her temples.

"I want you."

Stunned, she dropped her hands. "What?"

"I want you." Riley's eyes were molten gold and this time she didn't doubt him.

"But—but—why did we leave that other b-bed?" She stuttered on the words, no longer doubting, but still so surprised, she couldn't think straight.

"Even though Eric was gone, I wasn't sure who else might walk in at any moment." He advanced slowly, until she could feel his warm breath against her temple. "I wasn't sure if you knew what you were really asking for back there."

Eden swallowed. "Of course I do!"

His breath washed across her face again, and little tingles spread down her neck. "I wasn't sure if you knew what I was willing to give."

"And what's that?" she whispered, in her heart knowing he wouldn't say his love.

"An adventure. The excitement you were looking for when you left your library a few days ago."

Eden stared at the strong column of his throat, trying not to feel disappointed. Of course he wasn't offering love. "Don't you sound sure of yourself," she muttered.

"Not because I'm bragging." He lifted her chin with his crooked forefinger. "I can make that promise because of how you make me feel, Eden."

The melted gold of his eyes ran over her body. "And how is that?" she whispered.

"You make me feel like I can do everything right. Like I won't disappoint you. Like I can't fail." He drew his finger down, caressing the underside of her chin.

Eden couldn't catch her breath. Now that she was faced with what she'd thought she wanted—Riley in her arms—she was afraid. Making love with him wouldn't be about her body, it would be about her heart. Could she get that close to him and then walk away?

"I'll make it good for you, baby," he said huskily.

Her heart did an elevator fall to her toes. His seductive words, his seductive voice, made it impossible to say no. *Be honest with yourself, Eden.* She didn't want to say no. She might have only this one chance in life to make love with the man of her soul.

"I hope—I don't want to disappoint you—" Her fears about her inexperience came tumbling out.

He placed two fingers over her lips. "I'll make it good for you," he whispered.

And with that promise Eden abandoned her fears and abandoned her body to the man she loved.

He caught her tight to his chest, and she turned her cheek against his bare skin, smoothing her face over the firm muscle. The tiny nub of a male nipple hardened against her, and she instinctively sought it with her mouth. She kissed it, only a peck, really, yet still he groaned.

She looked up at him, surprised by his quick response. His eyes were closed, dark lashes feathered against his tanned cheeks. Still watching him, she ran her lips across his nipple. An expression—the physical manifestation of a sigh?—crossed his face. Her tongue darted out, tasted the hard nub, and his head dropped back, his eyes still squeezed shut.

Her heart clenched painfully, and she laved him again. No one, no book, no magazine, no movie, had ever explained the sweet pleasure-pain of pleasing the man you loved. She moved to his other nipple, sucked it lightly into her mouth.

"Eden."

He said just the one word, but it told her so much. She smiled against his skin, breathing him in, trying to imprint his feel, his fragrance in her memory.

"Eden." He tilted her chin, and crushed his mouth against hers.

What a kiss. Like the sunlight on the ocean, it dazzled her. Her mouth softened to let in his tongue, and she reveled in the freedom of the caress. Without deceptions or misgivings between them, without anything between them but her unspoken love, she could savor each sensation—each sweep of his tongue, each tingle that his mouth sent racing down her body.

He lifted his head, his breath dragging in and out raggedly. "What you do to me." He shook his head as if unable to explain.

She speared fingers through his long hair, brushing it away from his face. "What you do to me..." She smiled. "Do it some more."

He grinned. "Let's do it in the bedroom."

She cocked a saucy eyebrow, tamping down any nervousness. "That doesn't sound like an adventure," she teased.

He took her hand and walked backward toward the bedroom, drawing her with him. "But it's more comfortable," he said, his face turning serious. "For your first time."

Thump-thump-thump-thump. Eden's heart beat frantically as they crossed the threshold and moved toward the bed.

"Nervous, honey?" Riley paused, and cupped her cheek with his hand. "We don't have to, you know."

"Yes," she whispered. "We have to." Making love with him was what she wanted above all else.

With a tender smile, he sat down on the bed and pulled her closer. His hands went to the knotted sash of her robe. He fumbled a bit. "Damn," he said ruefully. "I'm shaking like a virgin." He looked up, aghast. "Oh, jeez, terrible choice of words."

Eden giggled, and held out both her hands. "But look at me, steady as a rock." They both ignored the fine trembling in her fingers.

The knot unloosed, and Riley pushed the robe off her shoulders. It hit the floor with a whisper of sound. He swung his legs onto the mattress and pulled her down beside him.

"Steady, baby, steady," he reminded her as she nervously plastered herself against him. He gently pushed away. "Let me see you in this lace thing again. A teddy, right? I was afraid to look for more than an instant last time."

A moment of silence, then he let out a low whistle of appreciation. "You make my heart stop," he said.

And you make mine nearly beat out of my chest, Eden thought. He ran a teasing finger over the thin straps and traced the neckline of the low-cut bodice. Her breath sped up as his finger took the same slow path again.

"I can't wait," he murmured, and then with a quick, deft movement, he jerked on the teddy's straps, peeling down the lace to completely reveal her breasts.

Eden's arms came up instinctively, but he just as quickly caught her hands to prevent them from shielding her. "Let me look," he said. "Since last night on the beach, I've fantasized about your breasts." Under his hot gaze, her nipples puckered. Embarrassment left Eden, replaced by an astonishing arousal. *Just from him looking at her!* She clenched her legs together as excitement feathered from her breasts to her abdomen.

His palms cupped her breasts, plumping them with caressing thumbs. "Mmm," he said appreciatively. Then he stroked the hard tips. "I want to taste them, feel them against my tongue." He switched his gaze to her face.

His words, his look, sent a blaze of wet heat coursing through her body. She swallowed. She couldn't feel her toes—they must have melted.

A smile creased his cheeks. "You should see your face. Like you're terrified and tantalized at the same time. Don't you like my mouth on you? You did last night."

Last night? What was he talking about? She could only think of today, this moment, *right now*. Without volition, her back arched, pressing her swelling breasts into his hands.

He chuckled knowingly. "Yes," he said, for some reason, and bent his head.

Yes. His mouth, hot and wet, claimed her nipple, sucked it in without preliminaries. A shard of pure desire flashed toward her belly. His big hands ran down her sides, grasped her hips and dragged her close against him. His pajama-clad leg moved between her thighs and pressed against her, *there*. She heard a moan, knew it was hers.

"So responsive," he murmured, then covered her other nipple. His tongue swirled around it, then took it in his mouth.

"Riley." She hardly recognized her own voice. Hoarse and needy, she knew it told him how close she was to the brink.

He lifted his head, and looked at her, his pupils dilated. "Slow down," he said. "We should slow down."

Eden tried to draw in a breath, but her heart was in her throat and desire was everyplace else. "I can't." She panted, feeling the pressure of his leg against the center of her. "Riley," she said again, asking him, pleading.

He closed his eyes and stilled. "Honey... slow... slow is..."

She ran her hands down his chest, feeling the muscles of his abdomen twitch as she reached the drawstring of his pajamas. "I want it, Riley. I want it—you—*now*." She couldn't wait a second longer.

In a burst of restrained movement, he gently pulled off the rest of her teddy and shucked his pajama bottoms. The drawer of the bedside table slid open and he pulled out a small packet. He quickly smoothed on the condom. When they came together again, bare inches of skin against bare inches of skin, he sighed with her. Their kiss was long and wet, and his furred leg slid again between her thighs. He pushed against her, and she pushed back. His mouth found her nipples again, and she clutched him to her.

He gently pushed her flat on her back, and still kissing her breasts, he parted her legs and put his hand against her soft folds. His mouth lifted at his first touch. She felt him gasp.

"So hot. So wet." He seemed so pleased, she dropped the last of her embarrassment and relaxed her legs. His fingers stroked her, and her breath caught. A finger filled her. She couldn't breathe. He moved it slowly, in and out, and his tongue filled her mouth in the same rhythm.

The stars came out behind her tightly squeezed eyes. A whole galaxy of stars born of desire. "Riley, Riley." She whispered his name and tried to draw him over her. Tingles pricked her scalp and goose bumps rioted over her flesh, all the way to her toes that still felt as though they'd melted into the mattress. And the warmth traveled up. Up, up, up her legs to pool in incredible heat as he filled her with a second finger. She whimpered.

His movements stilled. "Did I hurt you?"

She shook her head restlessly. "I *need* you."

"I know," he whispered.

The stars were whirling now, spinning in time with her out-of-control heartbeat. "Please, Riley."

"Yes, honey, yes."

His fingers left, left her wanting and panting with desire, and then a moment passed and he was between her legs, spreading them. She opened her eyes, and his incredibly handsome face filled her vision.

"I'm coming to you, baby." His voice was stark with need, his gold eyes watching her steadily.

She ran her hands down his back, her fingers tracing the heavy bumps of his spine. She caught hold of his hips, pulled him toward her, pulled him toward the place a woman needed the man she loved. *I have to make him part of me.*

Riley felt the urging of Eden's hands and tried to restrain himself. He wanted to plunge forward, to bury himself in her, but as hot and wet as she was, she was still a virgin. He probed her gently, pushed slowly. *Slowly, slowly,* he chanted to himself, breaking out in a sweat as her tight, tight body made way for him.

At the barrier, he felt her stiffen a little, and gasp. "Honey?" If it killed him, he'd pull away if that was what she wanted.

"Riley," she whispered, her pupils huge. "Come to me. Please."

A wash of chills ran over his back, then he pushed forward, watched her flinch as the barrier broke. His shaft sank in and with a groan he filled her mouth with his tongue.

Paradise.

He lay above her, her heartbeat pounding against his chest, her fragrance and the scent of arousal filling his head. He thought about drawing back, maybe drawing away altogether—how much was she hurting? But then she sucked lightly on his tongue, and he groaned again.

Though he tried to be gentle, he couldn't stop his hips from softly rocking. Within moments, her body was rocking back, bumping against him in an inexperienced rhythm.

It made him hot as hell.

He thought about ice cubes again, trying to think cold to counteract the delicious grip she had on his body, the terrifying hold she had on his heart. Her movements synced with his now, and he lifted his head to look into her eyes.

"You okay?" he whispered.

She nodded, and lifted her head from the pillow to kiss his shoulder.

The gentle touch of her lips on his flesh sent another wash of gooseflesh down his back. "You feel so good," he said, thrusting his body into her as tenderly as he could.

"More," she answered, her fingers splayed on his buttocks, holding him against her. "I want more."

Riley smiled around the pain of his accordioning heart. "I love how you respond to me," he whispered back. He rocked against her, pushing higher this time, watching her face for discomfort. Instead he saw arousal. Need.

"Come with me," he urged. Reaching down, he pulled her legs around his hips, felt her open wider. He moved against her slick skin, watched every nuance of pleasure pass over her expressive face. She gazed back, her eyes growing more heavy lidded, until they closed altogether.

He rose on his elbows and looked down at where their bodies joined. His heart constricted again, though he tried to tell himself it was only lust that made him so primitively satisfied to watch his body take hers.

He rubbed a thumb across her nipple, the feel of it like a sweet berry tempting him.

I've got to hold back, I've got to wait.

She arched up, and he took her breast in his mouth, the taste heating his blood, accelerating his thrusts, until he was no longer holding back but instead pressing forward, hoping she was with him, going there, there, *there.*

She jerked beneath him, her thighs clamping around his hips, and he groaned her name and spasmed, his hips driving into the cradle of her body. They trembled together, their lips meeting for a long, sweet kiss.

Tremors finally subsiding, he lay against the soft pillow, her hair beneath his cheek, and smelled the salt of the ocean, the scent of crushed flowers, the very fragrance of age-old temptation and satisfaction.

"I saw stars," she murmured, turning her face so their noses touched. "A Milky Way full of stars, spinning away like they'd been thrown by a slingshot." A little smile played over her face. "Wow."

Riley drew in a breath, still trying to recover. He didn't feel like smiling at all. "I saw Paradise," he said simply.

She blinked, then was silent for a moment. "Well, that makes sense." He felt her shrug. "After all, I'm Eden." She laughed softly.

"Yes," Riley agreed. He didn't find anything funny about the thought.

Eden snuggled back against the hard curve of Riley's body. He breathed evenly against her ear—*I guess men really do nod off after sex!* She smiled, thrilled by the sight of his long fingers cupping her breast. Despite what a less-besotted woman might term snores sounding in her ears, she'd never felt closer to anyone in her life.

A warm glow of happiness rushed from her head to her feet—she could finally feel her toes again—and she spooned closer, her eyelashes drifting down in adrenaline-edged contentment. *This is so good.*

"Stop wiggling." The disgruntled command rumbled against her ear.

"Grumpy, grumpy, grumpy." She looked over her shoulder and smiled.

"Hey, this is the best rest I've had since I met you, and I've only been sleeping all of about—" he lifted his head to read the bedside clock, then groaned "—ten minutes." He dropped his head onto the pillow with an audible *flump*. "Aren't you tired?"

"Tired? What do I need sleep for?" She felt like she'd downed a double espresso. "It's daylight and I'm in bed with the man I've just made love to." To communicate her enthusiasm, she wiggled back another time.

Riley edged away. "The man hounding you to do it again, if you keep that up."

Eden tilted back her head to meet his eyes. "Is that a problem?"

His hand tightened possessively over her breast. "Not for me, honey, but I'm thinking you might be a little sore."

"A little," she admitted.

"Then let's take a rest." Something in his voice told her he'd closed his eyes again.

She turned over to face him. "You're really going to sleep?"

He grunted.

"Can't we at least have some pillow talk?"

Riley's eyes opened. *"Pillow talk?"* He screwed up his face in exaggerated pain.

He was so sexily gorgeous, his golden eyes warm with humor. "You know. We just, uh, talk. You know. Intimately," she said.

Riley groaned.

She frowned. "Come on, Riley."

"I'll tell you what. I'll do the pillow and you do the talk." As if she'd agreed, he burrowed his head deeper and drew her closer against him, resting his cheek on her hair.

It was hard to argue with a cuddling man. She sighed, that feeling of happiness overwhelming her again. "I never thought it could be like this," she said, almost to herself.

"Hmm. Like what?"

She pressed her mouth against the side of his neck and breathed in his male scent. *Mmm.* "The closeness of this man and woman thing."

"Hmm." His arms tightened again and one of his thumbs stroked her spine.

Eden reveled in the flash flood of goose bumps that rushed down her body. "I think I didn't know, couldn't imagine, because my mother died when I was a little girl. When I was eight."

"Who raised you?"

"My father."

"Mmm. Me, too."

"Really?" With her forefinger, she traced little hearts on Riley's bare shoulder. "After my mother died, Daddy never romantically attached himself to anyone else. What about your father?"

"No."

Riley had tensed a little, so Eden didn't press him further. "Well, I didn't grow up with the example of a man and woman together. I think it stunted my growth," she said thoughtfully.

His big hand slid down her back and cupped her bottom. "If you ask me, you grew up just fine." There was a laugh in his voice.

"My *social* growth. And of course, Daddy has always been so protective of me."

"Daddy's little girl, huh?"

Eden traced her finger down his chest to his nipple, drew a tiny heart, then a fat, mushy one around it. "I guess. But I think it was more than that."

Riley suddenly became interested in her ear. "More?" he asked absently, the question just a rush of warm breath against her skin.

Eden tilted her neck so he could run his tongue around the edge of her ear. "I like that," she said throatily.

He took her earlobe between his teeth and bit gently. "You taste good."

She squirmed, arching her back to press closer to the hard heat of his body. "Riley..."

He laughed softly. "You're so easy, you know that?"

She pulled away to give him a mock glare. "Hey, that's not nice."

He feathered his fingers down her spine. "Ah, baby, but I think you're *not* such a nice girl." He wiggled his eyebrows and leaned forward to give her a teasing kiss on the nose. "Maybe that's what your daddy was so afraid of. That underneath her Miss Prim exterior, his dutiful daughter was really a vixen."

Eden laughed, delighted with the idea of Riley considering her a vixen. "No." She shook her head. "I think Daddy was more worried that men might be after our name or our money." And *she* knew the only man who could bring out the vixen in her was Riley.

His stroking fingers stilled. "What do you mean? Your name or your money?"

Eden grimaced. "You know, the Whitney name."

He pushed away to look down at her, his eyes wary. "I don't know. What are you talking about?"

Eden felt more than a little embarrassed. She'd made the comment like her family name was a household word. And though to many, she knew, it was, how horribly pompous of her to assume Riley was familiar with it. "My grandpapa Whitney made a lot of money in the 1920s."

Riley was looking at her like she'd turned from woman to wombat. "Whitney? As in *Whitney* Whitney?"

"Well, yes." She tried edging closer, but he inched away.

"Your father is *Ralph Waldo Whitney?*"

"Well, yes. Grandpapa had this literary thing going. My aunt is Jane Austen Whitney."

He didn't crack a smile. "Blue blood, highest social circles, fancy library-really-a-museum Whitney?"

"Yes." She swallowed, her mouth dry. "Is that—is that a problem for you?"

She took advantage of his stillness to close the inches of cool sheet between them. Her fingers brushed back his hair, and she felt more than a little desperate. Something was going on here, something she was afraid to understand. "Whitney... The Whitney name wouldn't affect our, uh, our... *adventure,* would it?"

Riley stared at her for long moments. Too-long moments. "Our adventure, you say?" The starch seemed to go out of him. "If all you're after is an adventure, baby, then I don't care what your name is." He pulled her closer to meet his mouth in a possessive, almost punishing, kiss.

10

Under the bright June sun, Riley lifted his hand for a final farewell wave to Nadine and Eric, unsuccessfully suppressing a disturbing mix of relief and anger. He was glad the *Getaway* team was gone, glad to end this sham of a honeymoon, but his guts roiled at the thought of the next goodbye.

His goodbye to Eden.

He glanced over at her, then made himself look away. But the golden strands of her hair lingered in his mind, as well as her sweet smile, and the newly awakened signs of passion in her eyes.

Groan.

He wanted to blame the whole damn mess on somebody—Miguel, Eden, anybody—but finger-pointing got him nowhere past himself. He was the one who'd become engaged to the totally wrong woman in the first place. He was the one who'd decided to play bride-and-groom with Eden. And then to take her to bed....

A pulsing ache of desire tightened his groin. *Damn, damn, damn.* To make love with a virgin-librarian-bluest-of-blue-bloods! A woman he could never hope to keep.

Had he completely lost his senses?

His hand automatically went to his pocket and gripped the wedding-band box, the one that he kept as a reminder. He ran his thumb over the velvet, trying not to compare the sensation to the feel of Eden's silky skin. *Remember.*

Riley Smith should stick with his own kind.

Riley Smith was not a marrying man.

"I don't like the way he was looking at me." Eden's voice interrupted his vow-taking.

"What?"

"The photographer. Eric. I don't like the way he was looking at me."

A hot, unnamed emotion spurted from Riley's heart to his tightly clenched hands. *"What do you mean?"* He forced his fingers open, then closed them carefully over her upper arm to pull her closer. "He didn't come on to you, did he?"

She shook her head, a worried wrinkle between her brows. "That wasn't it. He just—just seemed to recognize me."

He made himself release his grip, made himself let her go without even a lingering caress of her skin. "So what?" He was too close to her. The smell of her perfume invaded his head and made him think of their bed. *Oh, hell. Their* bed.

"What if he contacts my father?"

He didn't like her worried. He wanted to take her in his arms. Wanted to hold her against his heart and kiss away the frown. *Remember,* he told himself sternly. "So what if he does? If your daddy comes looking for you, you won't be here, right?"

She tilted her head, the frown still between her eyes.

"After tomorrow you'll be gone." He made himself say it. "Continuing on your adventure." *There wasn't another choice, right?*

"'After tomorrow you'll be gone.'" In the cozy back room of the resort's boutique, Eden repeated the sentence to Margarita. "Those were his exact words."

Shaking her head, Margarita tutted. "What is wrong with that foolish boy?" She looked up from the brilliantly colored caftan she was hemming. "I think you should shake him up and leave right this minute."

"This minute?" Eden's voice squeaked. Just the idea of leaving the man she loved felt like a hand clutching her throat.

"He is not appreciating you." Margarita shook her head again. "He is such a . . . such a *man.*"

"A man who's been hurt," Eden pointed out. "Remember, he was just jilted."

Margarita waved away the thought. "By one such as she, though. That shallow society girl didn't deserve my Riley."

Eden's gaze narrowed. "Shallow society girl? Who exactly was this woman?"

"Her first name, it is not worth remembering. But her last . . . Delaney, I think."

Delaney. She knew them by reputation. The hoity-toity family were legendary for the airs they put on. If she remembered right, her father had nothing good to say about Lawrence Delaney. "Do you think that Riley might be guilty of a little reverse-snobbery?"

Margarita paused, her needle poised over the raw silk. "What do you mean?"

"Riley just found out about my family. We're, um..."

The other woman nodded. "Old family, old money, yes?"

Eden grimaced. "How'd you guess?"

"You forget that I know clothes, Eden. I recognized the quality of yours, even if I did not applaud the style." She smiled softly, and her eyes focused on something in the distance. "And I know something of what you are going through."

"You do?"

Margarita nodded. "Mexico, my home country, is a land of vast differences. The jungles, the deserts. The wealthy, and the poor."

Eden settled back in her chair, fascinated by the softening of the other woman's face.

"My family, it, too, had much wealth, and a very old name. And pride. Aaah, my *papá* had much too much pride." Margarita's hands rested on the caftan in her lap. "He did not like it when his only daughter fell in love with one of the ranch's *vaqueros.*"

"You?" Eden guessed.

Margarita nodded. "Me. And the man I loved, he had much pride also. He did not want me to have less. It took many days, many, many tears, before he finally agreed to make me his wife." She looked at Eden, her eyes brilliant with tears. "But we had long, happy years of love together. And our Miguel."

Eden smiled and reached over to pat the older woman's knee. "You were lucky."

"Yes. And it should be so for you."

Eden nodded absently, mulling the situation over in her mind. Riley's condemning phrase came back to her. "After tomorrow you'll be gone." *After tomorrow.* Why had he said it like that? If he was so eager for her to leave, wouldn't he have insisted on an immediate goodbye?

She stood up, eager to seek him out. Where there was a chance, there was hope. Smiling at Margarita, she said, "So you think I should shake him up and leave now?"

"It would not be a bad idea."

Eden nodded. "I think you just may be right."

If it was the last thing she'd do, Eden was determined to get a rise out of Riley. She found him in his office, buried behind a computer and two piles of printouts. When she called his name, he peered at her from behind the monitor.

"Huh?" he grunted, blinking at her as if he'd forgotten who she was.

That made her even more determined. "I'm leaving," she said crisply.

"Sure, sure." He looked back at his computer screen quickly. "Tomorrow. Or in a few days." His gaze slid over her, then slid back off. "Stay as long as you like. I know you're on a vacation."

Eden pursed her lips. "I think I should go today."

"There's no reason for that," he protested, his gaze not leaving the monitor.

Eden wanted to stamp her foot in frustration. While he wasn't pushing her out the door, thank goodness, he wasn't exactly holding her close, either. "I thought you were eager to have me on my way."

His desk chair squeaked as he restlessly rolled it back and forth. "Uh, I just didn't want to take up more of your time. But you're welcome to stay, uh, as long as you want. Hang out at the pool. Go parasailing. Take scuba lessons."

Eden smiled to herself. So Mr. Go-Ahead-With-Your-Adventure didn't really find it so easy to say goodbye. "I think I'll leave right now."

He looked up this time to meet her eyes. "You mean in a few hours?"

"No. I mean right now."

"I don't want you to leave," he said.

Her eyebrows rose.

"Before you've had a nice lunch," he added hastily. "Let me order something for you—"

"Riley. It's five-thirty. I've had lunch."

"Oh." He frowned. "Who with?"

"Margarita."

"You could have asked me," he grumbled.

A small bubble of satisfaction rose within her. "You walked away after we said goodbye to Nadine and Eric," she pointed out. "I didn't think you needed me anymore."

Squeak, squeak went his chair in the silence.

"Have dinner with me," he finally said. "On the restaurant terrace in an hour."

The bubble of satisfaction grew bigger, but she couldn't resist prodding him once more. "I'll leave right after we eat."

"You'll leave after dark?"

She shrugged. "I have to go sometime."

"Right," he said, his voice noncommittal. "I know that."

For the next sixty minutes she readied herself for her last chance at Riley, locking the door of the suite's bathroom in case he came back himself. She showered, shampooed her hair twice. Her arms ached after the half hour it took to dry her hair, battling inexperience and the new hair length to achieve the "casual, tousled" look the stylist had promised would be easy.

It didn't end up looking great, but it *was* dry.

A hasty call to Margarita produced another dress—this one of knit the gold of Riley's eyes. Scoop-necked and sleeveless, it clung to her breasts and skimmed her hips, ending just above her ankles. A long slit up one side made her bare legs look long.

Her hand trembled as she brought her lipstick to her mouth. Her eyes looked dark and luminous, and her mouth already rosy. After deciding against adding more color, she bit her lips to darken them. She checked the clock. Fifteen minutes late.

Her heart beat to the fast rhythm of her steps as she strode to the restaurant. If he didn't come right out and ask her to stay tonight, she would leave. And it couldn't be any of this "if you want to" and "don't hurry off" stuff. It had to be a flat-out "Please stay." Not only did her pride demand it, but she knew that without it, he'd never admit that he really wanted her. Really needed her.

As promised, she found him on the terrace—wearing black jeans and a beige silk shirt. His back was to her, and on a whim she walked up quietly behind him and slipped her palms over his eyes.

She bent and whispered in his ear, "Guess who?"

Both his hands reached up and patted her hair, moved down to her shoulders, slid against her sides to her hips. "Eden," he said, not a hint of laughter in his voice.

She dropped her hands. "You're no fun." She moved around him to sit in the chair opposite.

"You think so?—" His words broke off and he stared.

So this is it, she thought. This was why there were twenty beauty and fashion magazines on the news-stands, why women spent hours on their appearance. To make him stare, just one time to see the words die in his throat when he looked at her, was worth every cramp in her fingers from holding the hairbrush, was worth every glob of mascara and skip in the lipliner line.

Then she almost laughed out loud. She remembered that she'd decided against the makeup after all. So what put that look on Riley's face wasn't what was *on* hers at all. It had to be what shone from her eyes. Passion. Need. *Love.*

"You smell good," he said hoarsely, his nostrils flaring.

She almost laughed again. She'd even forgotten perfume. "I'm not wearing anything but your soap and shampoo." A smile broke across her face, and she lifted one hand to briefly touch his. "I smell like you."

A waiter interrupted the moment with a plate of appetizers and chilled champagne. "What's all this?" she asked.

He lifted his glass. "To thank you."

She frowned, staring at the rising bubbles in her champagne. "So what are we toasting to? To gratitude? To the end of our honeymoon?"

"To the beginning—"

She jerked up her head, hoping.

"—of your adventure."

Disappointed again, Eden wet her lips and looked at the man she loved as if she could brand his image on her heart. A breeze kicked up and tangled his long hair. He held the delicate champagne glass in his strong hands, his long fingers curled around the crystal flute. *My heart is that fragile.* She willed him to understand. *Be careful with me.*

She cleared her throat. "To beginnings," she said, touching the brim of her glass to his. A tiny sip, cold and fizzy, slid down her throat. "I can't have more than half a glass."

"Why?"

She made herself say it aloud. "Because I'll be leaving after dinner."

"Why?"

Because you won't ask me to stay. Because you don't love me.

Riley slowly, carefully, set down his champagne glass. Ordinary sounds receded, until the clink of china and silverware gave way to the thumping cadence of her heart and the sound—yes, the *sound*—of the heated gold of Riley's eyes.

Like the crackle of far-off lightning, his look was a distant, yet thrilling threat. Her hand crept toward the heat, met his fingers across the table and held on.

"Stay with me tonight." He sounded as though he didn't want to say the words. "Give me another night, Eden."

She could afford no sense of satisfaction or victory. She felt only reprieved, and an unquenchable quiver of excitement. "Yes."

Sex was different in the dark.

The heavy drapes blocked out all the light. Riley's hand felt hot, insistent, leading her to the bed. Nerves already frayed now felt raw. When he touched her bare shoulder with his other hand, she jumped.

"What's the matter?" he asked. He sounded on edge, too.

"I can't see you," she complained.

A feather touch drew down her cheek. "All the better to feel you with."

Eden didn't laugh. In the darkness she felt more vulnerable. As if for some perverse reason he could suddenly see into her heart. He had her body, her soul; she didn't want him to take her pride, too.

"You scare me," he whispered.

She shivered. "You're reading my mind."

Riley put her hand on his chest, flattened the palm over his heartbeat. "See what you do to me."

Beneath her hand his heart pumped heavily. Her breath caught in her throat. "What do you want, Riley?"

"Take me to Paradise again," he said.

Love welled like tears. She swallowed her apprehension and let her hand walk down the buttons of his shirt to the placket of his jeans. "Follow me," she answered.

But he did all the leading. In the hot, exciting darkness, he drew off her clothes. His seemed to melt away. Eden felt wanton, her body splayed against the cool sheets, begging for his touch.

And Riley seemed to know how to answer every plea. She gasped, she writhed, she loved him with every inch of her body. Her hands explored him, too, boldly, because in the dark she could pretend the touch was accidental until she heard him gasp. Then she would follow the caress with another, and then with a kiss, and then with her tongue.

She touched him in ways, did things to him she'd only read about and never imagined could be so arousing. The taste of his skin lingered on her tongue. The sound of his harsh breathing was like a fire to her blood. "I want you," she said, to stop herself from confessing her love.

He moved, their limbs tangling in a new direction. And then she felt a new touch. *There.* Wet, soft, incredible.

"*Riley.*"

His tongue stroked her again. "Let me, angel. Let me love you."

She wished away the darkness. She wanted to see him. She wanted to know that it was just a man that made her body shake, made her cry out and nearly scream with the heart-bursting, soft-rough invasion.

She climaxed, her body trembling in waves of sensation, her mind reeling with the intimacy of it. He slid up her body and held her close against his still powerfully thudding heart. Then he moved away.

"Don't go!" The words burst from her, the very words she wanted more than anything to hear from him.

He laughed softly. "I'm not going anywhere, honey. Don't you know? I won't leave you."

She heard a drawer open and close, the rip of foil. In seconds he was back in her arms.

He kissed her, his hands moving to cup her breasts. "I can make you want it again."

What was he talking about? Though she'd almost drowned in sensation, until she had his body in hers, she'd never be satisfied. She pulled him over her. "Paradise is waiting."

They found their way there together. Panting after their slow return, Eden stared into the darkness, Riley's heartbeat beneath her ear. After her first experience that morning, she thought she'd understood about physical passion.

But in the darkness, in the vivid sensations of touch without sight, she'd learned more. Sex could be sweet, tender, fun and funny. Or sex could burn like white-hot lightning, electrifying the senses. And searing the heart with love.

He whispered her name like a question, his voice matching the rough caress of his callused hand down her side.

"I'm here," she said. *And I'm not leaving.*

* * *

In the morning neither one mentioned Eden's departure from the Casa Luna. The idea barely crossed Eden's mind. They woke up, showered together, found their way back to bed. Riley, worried about the soreness of her body, was gentle until she raked him with her fingernails and lightly bit his shoulder.

By lunchtime, they'd found their way to the lagoon pool. They shared a lounge chair, Eden leaning back against Riley's chest. Miguel walked by, and his eyebrows nearly hit his hairline. "Ignore him," Riley ordered.

She was too tired to do anything but. She dropped her head against Riley's shoulder and her eyelids drifted closed. He kissed her temple and she let sleep swallow her up.

"Eden." Riley jostled her awake. "Eden. Someone's here to see you."

Her eyes lazily opened. Her brow pleated in confusion. "Someone to see me?"

She focused on the legs in front of her. Legs clad in a summer-weight wool suit. Expensive wool suit. She looked up. "Daddy?"

"Eden Marie." Her father's bald pate shone in the sunlight. She focused on that, not on the incredulous expression on his face. "I had a call. From *Getaway* magazine. A photographer said he suddenly remembered where he'd seen you before. *And they wanted a quote from me on your marriage.*"

His hand went into his pocket, and Eden heard his habitual, annoying, jangling of keys. "What is this place? What are you doing here? And who is this man?'' He ticked off his questions as if they were bulleted lines on a business memo.

Eden gaped, still trying to determine if this was real or a naptime nightmare.

Riley extricated himself from behind her, and stood to hold out his hand to her father. ''Mr. Whitney. I'm Riley Smith.''

Her father ignored Riley and his outstretched hand. *''Eden?''*

While her father could be annoyingly protective, he was rarely rude. ''Daddy!'' Eden said, shocked.

Her father frowned. ''I'd like to know exactly what's going on here.''

''I'm on a vacation. You know that.''

''With this—this—'' Her father gestured to Riley, who seemed to have turned to stone. ''This *gigolo?*''

That brought Riley to life. His hands fisted at his sides. ''Excuse me, but—''

''Let me talk to him alone, Riley,'' Eden interjected. She didn't want anything more said that might permanently destroy a chance of a friendship between the two men. She looked up at him, pleading. ''Please.''

With an angry shake of his head, Riley stalked off.

Eden stared at his stiff, retreating back. ''Daddy, how could you?''

''How could I what?'' Jangle, jangle went his keys. ''How could I come looking for my daughter when I hear that she's married? How could I be concerned that she may have attached herself to some smooth talker only out for her money?''

"Daddy, *please*. Just hold on a minute." She rubbed a hand across her forehead, trying to figure out where to begin. "Tell me again. How did you know where to find me?"

Jangle. "The travel magazine that published the article on the library a few months back. They called for a quote on your marriage. To a *bartender*."

Eden's stomach churned. "What did you say, Daddy?" Could he have possibly blown the *Getaway* coverage for the Casa Luna?

Her father gestured brusquely. "What I always say when I don't have all the facts. 'No comment.'"

"Thank goodness." Her stomach calmed.

"Thank goodness? Is that all you have to say? Are you married or are you not?"

Eden rubbed her forehead again. "Daddy—"

"And that swimsuit! In God's name, what kind of place is this?"

"Daddy." She realized she had to take a firm stand now. Rising from the chair, she spoke in her calmest, most reasonable voice. "I'm not married to Riley, but I'd appreciate another 'No comment,' if anyone else asks you about it."

His eyes narrowed shrewdly. "Why shouldn't I deny such a ludicrous idea?"

"Because I asked you to."

Her father crossed his arms over his chest. "Not good enough."

"Please, Daddy."

"Only if you come home with me right now."

"What?"

He didn't blink. "I won't say anything if you come home with me right now. Otherwise, I call that magazine and tell them this marriage is a hoax."

Riley set Eden's suitcases by the front door of the suite just as the door opened, clipping him in the forehead. "Eden."

She gasped, and reached up. He flinched away. He couldn't let her touch him now. The pain in his head was nothing compared to what was going on in his heart.

"Are you okay?" she asked.

"Just ducky." It wasn't every day that he was accused of being a gigolo.

She stepped farther into the room and closed the door. Her glance caught on the suitcases, and she stilled. "What's this?"

"Your stuff."

She bit her lip. "I can see that," she said slowly. "Is this about my father? Listen, I'm sor—"

"It has nothing to do with your father," he lied. "I know you wanted to get on with your vacation, and so I thought I'd hurry things along."

"Hurry *me* along, you mean."

He shrugged.

"Riley." She came forward again, and he stepped back. *"Riley."*

He steeled himself against the look on her face. "It's time, Eden," he said. "It's been fun, but—" he shrugged "—it's over."

Now she stepped back, as if he'd physically pushed her away. "I know it's about my father," she whispered. "But let me—"

"It's about you, Eden." He whirled to stare out the window, to watch a wave roll inevitably toward the shore. "What was between us, it couldn't last."

"Why?" Her voice sounded quieter than the muffled *shush* of the faraway wave against the sand. "I won't go until—*unless* you can tell me why." He could tell she meant it.

He looked out toward the horizon, the ocean a field of blue-gray that he wished he could walk away on. "I'm a bastard," he admitted.

A small pause. "Well, you're acting like a jerk right now, but I wouldn't say—"

Turning toward her, he let out a harsh bark of laughter. "No, Eden, I mean a *real* bastard, as in mother and father unmarried."

She blinked. "Something tells me this is more than a controversy over whose last name to use."

He laughed again, if the raw sound that came from his throat could be called that. "Yeah."

"I'm listening."

"My mother was sixteen years old when she crossed over to the wrong side of the tracks for some fun. And I guess you could say she found a little too much. She got pregnant by my dad, your typical nineteen-year-old bowling alley janitor." An image of his father flashed in Riley's mind. A young man who died old, hard and bitter, of bad luck and bad liquor.

"And they didn't marry?" Eden asked.

"They didn't even cohabit. Her parents found out when it was too late to get rid of me. So they just waited until I was born. Handed the baby over to the no-good janitor."

"So your father raised you?"

"Until he drank himself to death when I was fourteen."

A pained expression crossed Eden's sweet face. "Then what happened?"

"Then I raised myself."

"Your mother, her family, didn't know about your father's death?"

He laughed again. "Oh, yeah, they knew. They even came to our apartment to take a look at me. I hadn't had a haircut in a few months. I hadn't been to school in a few months, either."

"You poor little kid."

He shrugged off the emotion in her voice. "That's not how they saw it. They were ashamed to admit they'd watered down their bloodlines by producing a lowlife like me."

"What do you mean?"

"They refused to take me to their side of the tracks."

"Riley." Anger filled her voice. "That's disgusting."

"Yeah, it is, isn't it?" He turned again to stare back at the ocean. "Right then I made a vow that I should never have forgotten. Stay away from blue bloods. Stick with my own kind."

"But—but I'm not like that."

He wouldn't turn around. He wouldn't look into her face. "Listen, Eden, I'm an uneducated guy from the other side of the tracks. You're a privileged little rich girl. Just like my mom and dad, we had our little fling. Let's not take it any further."

"But you *know* me. I'm not . . . I don't . . ."

He couldn't take it anymore. He just wanted her gone so he could start forgetting. Whirling, he met her gaze. "Don't you get it? I don't trust this." He gestured to indicate the passion that ran between them. "I don't trust *you.*"

She flinched as if he'd struck her. He watched her swallow, and the movement appeared to pain her. "It's not fair," she said in a confused voice.

He smiled. "I'm sorry to break it to you, honey, but life is never that."

She looked about wildly, as if unsure what to do or where to go. Her gaze snagged on her suitcases. She grabbed them up, practically ran out the door. It closed with an anticlimactic click.

The wood was so thick, Riley couldn't even hear her footsteps running away, though he listened for a long time. "Paradise lost," he finally whispered.

11

Miguel shook his head at Riley. "I've said it before, I'll say it again. You're a nut case."

Riley ignored his partner's diagnosis. "Just keep your eyes open. If you see her, we're going to have to hightail it outta here." He'd dragged Miguel to a public exhibition of still life art in the gardens of the Whitney Library.

"I thought that was the whole reason why we're here. You haven't seen Eden in three weeks and you can't get through another day without assuring yourself she's still breathing."

"Damn it, Miguel, don't be intentionally dense. We want to catch sight of *her,* but she can't catch sight of *us.*"

"Maybe we should have chosen less noticeable disguises." Miguel pushed up the brim of his white Panama hat. "Though I think I have a distinctly 'Miami Vice' appeal in this thing."

Riley reached over and batted down the brim of Miguel's hat, then readjusted his own soft fisherman's cap. "These aren't disguises, they're just . . . just . . ."

"Stupid? Ridiculous? Sil—"

"Shh." Riley averted his eyes from an older couple who walked by, looking at them curiously. The hats had seemed like a good idea at the time, but the wooded grounds of the library were plenty shady, something that the hundreds of people milling around the artwork had apparently been aware of. With the exception of an old lady in a Jackie O. pillbox carrying a Queen Elizabeth handbag, they were the only two in headgear.

"There she is."

Miguel's words caused Riley to gaze about in a panic. "Where—where—" *Oh.* He inhaled a long breath. *Ah.*

He exhaled in relief. She hadn't seen them. She sat at a table, fifty feet away, chatting with the old lady in the pillbox. He hadn't dreamed Eden. There she was, the same. The same beautiful eyes, nose, ears. The same sweet mouth he remembered tasting....

His blood pumped heavily to his groin. God, how it ached to remember.

"She looks weird."

Riley looked at Miguel, annoyed. "What the hell do you mean by that?"

Miguel took a half step back. "Take it easy. What I mean is, she looks like she did when I first met her. Now, don't get mad, but she looks kind of...frumpy."

"Frumpy?"

"Yeah. Not at all like the woman that I saw on the last day she was at the Casa. That woman was vibrant looking, happy...."

"Ready for an adventure?" Riley looked back at Eden. Dressed in a long gray dress and sensible shoes, her hair pulled back in a low ponytail, Miguel was right. She looked like *she* was the one in disguise.

"Do you think she's sick?" he asked Miguel.

"Lovesick."

Riley rolled his eyes. "Seriously."

"Hell, Riley, I *am* being serious. And I think you're sick in the head."

"So you've said." Riley paced over to an empty wrought-iron bench from where he could still see Eden.

"Well, maybe you should start listening to me."

Riley grunted.

"Yeah, go all Neanderthal on me, just like you always do when you don't want to listen. But I'm gonna tell you anyway. Why do you think you and Eden can't be together—"

"You *know* why."

Miguel snorted. "Oh, yeah. You're from two different worlds and never the two shall marry. You're nachos and she's oysters—"

"She hates oysters," Riley interjected absently.

Miguel threw up his hands. "There you go, then! You see how dumb your reasons against her are."

"You can't understand."

"You think so?" Miguel continued stubbornly. "You're wrong. My mother's family was rich, my father had nothing."

Riley's eyebrows rose. "Margarita and your father? She claims they had a marriage made in heaven."

"They did. She left behind her family. Left behind their money and their disapproval to come to California with my father. They started with nothing—never had much more than that, really. But they were the happiest couple on earth until the day *Papá* died."

Riley sat quietly on the bench, the people passing back and forth in his vision not even registering. Then a figure stopped before him. "Riley Smith," a man said. "I'm right, am I not?"

Riley stood up and automatically held out his hand before realizing the man was Eden's father, the Daddy Warbucks look-alike, Ralph Waldo Whitney.

Mr. Whitney gave Riley's hand a punishing shake. "Good to see you." His voice was hearty. "Are you here to meet Eden?"

Riley blinked in surprise. "Uh, no, sir."

"Ah." The man's face registered disappointment. "I'm, uh, sorry to hear that."

Riley blinked again.

"Goodbye, then." The man turned to walk away, then quickly turned back. "I threatened to call the magazine, you know. Did she tell you that? I told her if she didn't return with me immediately I'd tell them it was a hoax."

Riley didn't know what to say.

The older man shook his bald head. "She called my bluff. Said she'd do as she pleased, thank you very much, and left me standing by that pool." He shook his head again. "She never would have done that in the past." He shot Riley an assessing look. "Though a few minutes later she found me and said she was coming home after all."

He took a few steps away, then turned. "Strange, how you don't want them to grow up, but when they do, you never want them to go back." Mr. Whitney looked over his shoulder in the direction of Eden. "The woman I glimpsed for a moment I miss more than the little girl I remember." This time he left and didn't return.

Miguel stood up, prodded Riley with a sharp elbow. "Now what are you going to do?"

Riley took a long look at Eden.

And a realization engulfed him, exploding air from his lungs, crushing him like a tidal wave crushing the sand.

He loved her.

He loved every frumpish-adventurous-innocent-passionate thing about her. He loved how sweetly she smiled, how gently she reached out to people, to life. How strongly she'd clung to him when they'd made love.

She deserved the best. The very best.

Miguel prodded him again. "What are you going to do?" he repeated.

Riley took another long look at Eden. Took a longer look inside his worthless soul. He stuck his hand in his pants pocket and ran his fingers over the wedding-band box, that reminder of his vows. "Nothing."

Miguel rolled his eyes. "A nut case. I said it before, and I'll say it again...."

Riley didn't hear anything more, just the sad, slow beat of his heart.

Eden stared at the forest of newly sharpened pencils on her desktop. *If only I could hate the man.* Wouldn't that make the long, lonely days easier?

Couldn't she then forget the memories that made her ache with desire in the dark hours of the night?

"What's on your docket for today?" The overly hearty voice of her father broke into her thoughts.

"Same as yesterday." And the day before that, and the day before that. The same as every day for the past four weeks, A.R. After Riley.

An unfamiliar expression crossed over her father's face. Uncertainty? Indecision? "You know, all these years I've been so busy worrying about the men not good enough for you, that I never thought to warn you about the men who didn't *think* they were good enough for you."

Eden frowned. That was the longest speech on male-female relations that she'd ever heard from her father. But before she could question him about it, he walked quickly away, as if he'd already said too much.

She watched after him curiously. Since her return from the Casa Luna, he'd tiptoed around her like he was on eggshells. She knew he regretted his try at manipulating her, just as she'd known he would never have gone against her request and actually contacted *Getaway.* Her father loved her.

If only Riley did.

The traitorous thought came to her, along with another twist of pain in her heart. *Damn him, damn him, damn him.* The words didn't make her feel the least bit better.

The sound of footsteps caught her attention. Her father returned to her desk. "One more piece of advice?"

Astonished again, she nodded.

"Listen to someone who has seen a little more of the world than you, Eden." An odd expression crossed her father's face and he cleared his throat. "To someone who had some investigating done of Riley Smith. When you think about Riley, and what might be going through his mind, consider what it would be like to be ashamed of things you've done . . . or things you haven't done. Or worse, what it would be like to feel that the person you loved was ashamed of *you.*"

She opened her mouth to protest. To assure him that she didn't—couldn't—feel the least ashamed of Riley and what he had done or hadn't done. But as she watched her father's retreating back, she replayed what he'd said. What if Riley *thought* she could be ashamed of him?

She tried rejecting the thought. But it popped up in her head, over and over. *Humph.* She crossed her arms over her chest. He should have had more faith in her. He should have fought against his prejudices! Yes, he should have fought for her!

Like I should have fought for him.

Wouldn't that be what a *real woman* did? Wouldn't a woman go out on a limb for the man who made her feel adventurous? Shouldn't she take a page from Riley's book and get herself a little attitude?

For some stupid, sentimental reason, Riley had yet to move out of the honeymoon suite he'd shared with Eden at the Casa Luna. The maids vacuumed, scrubbed, and changed the sheets daily, but he could still smell her fragrance in the air. He would leave when the scent was gone, he promised himself.

He walked from the rooms to the restaurant's terrace for breakfast, absently waving his unrolled newspaper at the staff and guests who greeted him. Once seated at the table, he sat back and opened his paper. The waitress would bring orange juice, coffee and the chef's daily special, just like she had every day since Eden left.

Now that it was July, the early-morning sunshine was even brighter, the blue of the sky and the sound of the ocean making the Casa even more like Paradise.

Paradise. Why had he even thought the word? Like a sneaky, persistent thief, it kept cropping up in the dialogue of his mind. Each time it brought kaleidoscope images of Eden: her smile, her eyes, the sweet curve of her lush mouth. Each time it stole away a piece of his sanity. Maybe Miguel was right. He *was* a nut case.

To fight the memories, he unrolled the newspaper. He idly turned the sheets, pausing to read the articles that caught his attention. Suddenly he looked up, a sixth sense telling him that something was wrong...or different.

Where's Andrea with my orange juice? Where is everyone else? While an early breakfast was not the norm at the Casa Luna, usually someone would be sharing the terrace.

He tossed aside the front pages and moved to the Business section of the paper. Concentrating on the words was so hard, he almost gave up, but he made himself check the NASDAQ, then turned one last page. His eyes nearly popped out of his head. There was his name. Three inches high. In the middle of a full-page ad.

> Eden Marie Whitney, daughter of
> Ralph Waldo Whitney, Esq.
> loves
> Riley Smith, barkeep, hotelier,
> all-around wonderful man.
> We've had the honeymoon and
> I want it to last forever.

P.S. To let you know I'd admit this to anybody, this ad is being run in every newspaper in every major city in North America.

P.P.S. If you make up your mind quick, you can be my date for the wedding of the youngest Delaney daughter to the family's head gardener.

A swath of chills ran over Riley's back. He looked around the terrace, expecting Miguel to pop out and admit to a sicko practical joke. But the tables were still deserted.

A breeze kicked up, and the fragrance of...of Eden swirled around his head. He looked behind him, looked toward the terrace entrance, then over the balcony.

"Here I am."

Her voice. From the door to the kitchen Eden emerged, a tall glass of orange juice in her hand. She set it in front of him and joined him at the table.

Astounded, by the ad and the vision of Eden herself in a short, flirty dress, Riley couldn't say a word.

His mouth moved, his mind whirled, but not one coherent thought formed.

Eden gestured to the paper. "She didn't jilt you for any other reason than that, you know."

He swallowed, still trying to get his mind on track. "Than what?"

"Love." Eden laced her fingers together and stared at them, just as she had the first time they'd sat across from each other, in Riley's No. 1. "I ... happened to call her and she told me the whole story. She'd fallen in love with the family gardener years ago."

"I see," Riley said, and he did. He knew what it was like to try to forget someone you loved.

"Without you, I'm no good, Riley." She bit her lip. "I just go back to my old musty, dusty librarian ways."

He hardly heard her. He could only think how absolutely impossible it was to forget someone you loved.

"Is there a way I could make you trust me? A way I could make you believe I won't ever want anyone but you?"

Her questions came to him from a distance. His mind was focused on the words of the ad. *Eden Marie Whitney ... loves Riley Smith....*

She'd written it for all the world to see.

Not the least bit ashamed.

Not the least bit afraid to risk her heart.

He tried swallowing the lump in his throat. And she thought she wasn't adventurous.

How could he possibly deserve such a woman? How could she possibly want him?

And yet, and yet, here she was, offering a chance as limitless as the Paradise blue of the sky.

Wasn't it time to get his guts up and grab her, just like he had everything else he'd really ever wanted?

Why be so afraid of this exhilarating, intoxicating, *happy* feeling? Why not take a real risk and go for love?

Eden was an adventurous, loving woman. And he'd made a vow to stick with his own kind.

"What?" He looked up, the catch in her voice snagging his attention. "What did you say?"

She swallowed. "I asked you what you thought of my ad."

"Pretty exciting stuff," he said, his gaze not leaving her face.

And it was easy to tell what she read on his, because her lips curved upward in an incredulous smile. Love shone from her eyes. "That's the kind of woman I am," she said, a laugh in her voice.

He reached over to grab her hand and drew her toward him, onto his lap. "*My* kind of woman." He kissed her mouth, her eyes, her ears, every inch of skin he could reach. God, she felt so good in his arms. "I love you," he said, his voice hoarse. "So much."

"And I love you," she whispered back.

Out of his pocket he fished the jeweler's box with the wedding band he'd been holding on to all this time. He stared down at it, ran his thumb over the now-worn velvet top. He gave Eden another tender kiss, then curled back his arm and threw the damn thing over the balcony and into the ocean.

"What *was* that?" Eden asked, her fingers stroking his face.

"Just a reminder."

"Of what?"

"I don't remember."

And the sun shone bright, and the sea gulls shrieked, and the waves took their inevitable path to the shore, as inevitable and endless as the love that Riley Smith felt for Eden Marie Whitney.

*   *   *   *   *

1

Morgan Brigham slowly set down his coffee cup on the kitchen table and stared at the comic strip in the center of his paper. It was nestled in among approximately twenty others that were spread out across two pages. But this was the only one he made a point of reading faithfully each morning at breakfast.

This was the only one that mirrored *her* life.

He read each panel twice, as if he couldn't trust his own eyes. But he could. It was there, in black and white.

Morgan folded the paper slowly, thoughtfully, his mind not on his task. So Traci was getting engaged.

The realization gnawed at the lining of his stomach. He hadn't a clue as to why.

He had even less of a clue why he did what he did next.

Abandoning his coffee, now cool, and the newspaper, and ignoring the fact that this was going to make him late for the office, Morgan went to get a sheet of stationery from the den.

He didn't have much time.

"What do you think, Jeremiah? Too blunt?"

The dog, part bloodhound, part mutt, idly looked up from his rawhide bone at the sound of his name. Jeremiah gave her a look she felt free to interpret as ambivalent.

"Fine help you are. What if Daniel actually reads this and puts two and two together?"

Not that there was all that much chance that the man who had proposed to her, the very prosperous and busy Dr. Daniel Thane, would actually see the comic strip she drew for a living. Not unless the strip was taped to a bicuspid he was examining. Lately Daniel had gotten so busy he'd stopped reading anything but the morning headlines of the *Times*.

Still, you never knew. "I don't want to hurt his feelings," Traci continued, using Jeremiah as a sounding board. "It's just that Traci is overwhelmed by Donald's proposal and, see, she thinks the ring is going to swallow her up." To prove her point, Traci held up the drawing for the dog to view.

This time, he didn't even bother to lift his head.

Traci stared moodily at the small velvet box on the kitchen counter. It had sat there since Daniel had asked her to marry him last Sunday. Even if Daniel never read her comic strip, he was going to suspect something eventually. The very fact that she hadn't grabbed the ring from his hand and slid it onto her finger should have told him that she had doubts about their union.

Traci sighed. Daniel was a catch by any definition. So what was her problem? She kept waiting to be struck by that sunny ray of happiness. Daniel said he wanted to take care of her, to fulfill her every wish. And he was even willing to let her think about it before she gave him her answer.

Guilt nibbled at her. She should be dancing up and down, not wavering like a weather vane in a gale.

Pronouncing the strip completed, she scribbled her signature in the corner of the last frame and then sighed. Another week's work put to bed. She glanced at the pile of mail on the counter. She'd been bringing it in steadily from the mailbox since Monday, but the stack had gotten no farther than her kitchen. Sorting letters seemed the least heinous of all the annoying chores that faced her.

Traci paused as she noted a long envelope. Morgan Brigham. Why would Morgan be writing to her?

Curious, she tore open the envelope and quickly scanned the short note inside.

Dear Traci,
I'm putting the summerhouse up for sale. Thought you might want to come up and see it one more time before it goes up on the block. Or make a bid for it yourself. If memory serves, you once said you wanted to buy it. Either way, let me know. My number's on the card.

Take care,
Morgan

P.S. Got a kick out of *Traci on the Spot* this week.

Traci folded the letter. He read her strip. She hadn't known that. A feeling of pride silently coaxed a smile to her lips. After a beat, though, the rest of his note seeped into her consciousness. He was selling the house.

The summerhouse. A faded white building with brick trim. Suddenly, memories flooded her mind.

Traci folded the letter. He read her strip. She hadn't known that. A feeling of pride silently coaxed a smile to her lips. After a beat, though, the rest of his note seeped into her consciousness. He was selling the house.

The summerhouse. A faded white building with brick trim. Suddenly, memories flooded her mind. Long, lazy afternoons that felt as if they would never end.

Morgan.

She looked at the far wall in the family room. There was a large framed photograph of her and Morgan standing before the summerhouse. Traci and Morgan. Morgan and Traci. Back then, it seemed their lives had been permanently intertwined. A bittersweet feeling of loss passed over her.

Traci quickly pulled the telephone over to her on the counter and tapped out the number on the keypad.

* * * * *

Look for TRACI ON THE SPOT
by Marie Ferrarella, coming to
Silhouette YOURS TRULY
in March 1997.

MILLION DOLLAR SWEEPSTAKES
OFFICIAL RULES
NO PURCHASE NECESSARY TO ENTER

1. To enter, follow the directions published. Method of entry may vary. For eligibility, entries must be received no later than March 31, 1998. No liability is assumed for printing errors, lost, late, non-delivered or misdirected entries.

   To determine winners, the sweepstakes numbers assigned to submitted entries will be compared against a list of randomly, preselected prize winning numbers. In the event all prizes are not claimed via the return of prize winning numbers, random drawings will be held from among all other entries received to award unclaimed prizes.

2. Prize winners will be determined no later than June 30, 1998. Selection of winning numbers and random drawings are under the supervision of D. L. Blair, Inc., an independent judging organization whose decisions are final. Limit: one prize to a family or organization. No substitution will be made for any prize, except as offered. Taxes and duties on all prizes are the sole responsibility of winners. Winners will be notified by mail. Odds of winning are determined by the number of eligible entries distributed and received.

3. Sweepstakes open to residents of the U.S. (except Puerto Rico), Canada and Europe who are 18 years of age or older, except employees and immediate family members of Torstar Corp., D. L. Blair, Inc., their affiliates, subsidiaries, and all other agencies, entities, and persons connected with the use, marketing or conduct of this sweepstakes. All applicable laws and regulations apply. Sweepstakes offer void wherever prohibited by law. Any litigation within the province of Quebec respecting the conduct and awarding of a prize in this sweepstakes must be submitted to the Régie des alcools, des courses et des jeux. In order to win a prize, residents of Canada will be required to correctly answer a time-limited arithmetical skill-testing question to be administered by mail.

4. Winners of major prizes (Grand through Fourth) will be obligated to sign and return an Affidavit of Eligibility and Release of Liability within 30 days of notification. In the event of non-compliance within this time period or if a prize is returned as undeliverable, D. L. Blair, Inc. may at its sole discretion, award that prize to an alternate winner. By acceptance of their prize, winners consent to use of their names, photographs or other likeness for purposes of advertising, trade and promotion on behalf of Torstar Corp., its affiliates and subsidiaries, without further compensation unless prohibited by law. Torstar Corp. and D. L. Blair, Inc., their affiliates and subsidiaries are not responsible for errors in printing of sweepstakes and prize winning numbers. In the event a duplication of a prize winning number occurs, a random drawing will be held from among all entries received with that prize winning number to award that prize.

5. This sweepstakes is presented by Torstar Corp., its subsidiaries and affiliates in conjunction with book, merchandise and/or product offerings. The number of prizes to be awarded and their value are as follows: Grand Prize — $1,000,000 (payable at $33,333.33 a year for 30 years); First Prize — $50,000; Second Prize — $10,000; Third Prize — $5,000; 3 Fourth Prizes — $1,000 each; 10 Fifth Prizes — $250 each; 1,000 Sixth Prizes — $10 each. Values of all prizes are in U.S. currency. Prizes in each level will be presented in different creative executions, including various currencies, vehicles, merchandise and travel. Any presentation of a prize level in a currency other than U.S. currency represents an approximate equivalent to the U.S. currency prize for that level, at that time. Prize winners will have the opportunity of selecting any prize offered for that level; however, the actual non U.S. currency equivalent prize if offered and selected, shall be awarded at the exchange rate existing at 3:00 P.M. New York time on March 31, 1998. A travel prize option, if offered and selected by winner, must be completed within 12 months of selection and is subject to: traveling companion(s) completing and returning of a Release of Liability prior to travel; and hotel and flight accommodations availability. For a current list of all prize options offered within prize levels, send a self-addressed, stamped envelope (WA residents need not affix postage) to: MILLION DOLLAR SWEEPSTAKES Prize Options, P.O. Box 4456, Blair, NE 68009-4456, USA.

   For a list of prize winners (available after July 31, 1998) send a separate, stamped, self-addressed envelope to: MILLION DOLLAR SWEEPSTAKES Winners, P.O. Box 4459, Blair, NE 68009-4459, USA.

You're About to Become a

Privileged Woman

Reap the rewards of fabulous free gifts and benefits with proofs-of-purchase from Silhouette and Harlequin books

Pages & Privileges™

It's our way of thanking you for buying our books at your favorite retail stores.

PROOF OF PURCHASE YT-PP22

Offer expires March 31, 1997

Pages & Privileges ™

TM

**Harlequin and Silhouette—
the most privileged readers in the world!**

For more information about Harlequin and Silhouette's PAGES & PRIVILEGES program call the Pages & Privileges Benefits Desk: 1-503-794-2499

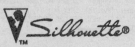

Silhouette®
TM

YT-PP2